GRACE'S Beast

GRACE'S *Beast*

THE *Lucent* CHRONICLES #1

Published by
TWO REALMS PUBLISHING LLC
HTTPS://TWO-REALMS-PUBLISHING-LLC.COM/
ISBN: 978-1-7346375-6-4

Cover and Interior Design: We Got You Covered Book Design
Editor: Cassandra Fear

TWOREALMS
PUBLISHING

Printed in the United States of America

GRACE'S *Beast*

THE *Lucent* CHRONICLES

BRIGIT ROSÉ

A tale as old as time. Brigit Rosé

To Mom.

Thank you for always being my advocate.

CHAPTER *one*

VINCENT'S GRIP ON his coffee mug tightened until his knuckles turned white. He cracked his neck and ground his teeth.

Nothing but their memory replayed in his mind. As if that was all his parents were. Just a memory.

Yes, they had died in a car crash nearly eleven years ago, but his parents meant more than just some cockamamie words on paper. Their story was more than whoever had written this… garbage! That's exactly what it was, pure and utter garbage. He didn't care how accurate the details were. His parents deserved more than what whoever had spewed this crap had given them.

That was the problem. He didn't know who had written this junk novel laid out before him.

The answer wouldn't be any different this time than it had been any other time since he had gone back to the front of the manuscript, but he did it again, anyway. Vincent stared at the space where "written by" should—no, would—have normally appeared.

Except there was nothing.

No "written by." No "by." Nothing to help him determine the novel's author. Of course, all of this had been on purpose. It was all part of the stupid competition his company ran annually. The one used to find new artists eager to have a publishing deal of any kind. Not that it was necessarily a poor offer: ten grand and a one-book publishing contract. The first two authors they'd signed had seen splendid success. Not so much with the last one.

But of all the entries he had read, none of them had ever been a story about his family… his parents… him.

And this one was just that.

It was *his* story, which made it his responsibility to make sure it never saw the light of day. No matter what.

Vincent banged his fist on the polished cherry oak desk and knocked the pen holder to the floor. Pens scattered across the plush, gunmetal gray carpet. Yanking the phone from its cradle, he depressed the button for his assistant.

"Get in here, now!" he screamed into the line and slammed the phone back down. Shit, he had to get himself under control. He couldn't let his other side come out. Inhaling and exhaling a couple of deep breaths, he mentally chanted the mantra *I am the calm before a storm.*

Burying his face into his hands, he groaned and dragged a hand through his dirty blond hair. Vincent hung his head and gripped the back of his neck. He could easily stop this manuscript from going forward without having to find out who authored it.

No. He had to find out. Whoever had written this story knew too much about his heritage, and that left him vulnerable. He had to know who they were and how they had found out so much about his… abilities.

Vincent stood, rising to his full height. He straightened the deep red tie at his throat, the black jacket across his broad shoulders, the black pants around his waist and crossed over to the view his office offered him of *the city*. His office sat a good hundred-feet high with a large bay window. From his vantage point, he could see the white flakes as they danced across the sky and blanketed the ground. One of the many things he enjoyed about the winter months. The cooler air also felt good against his preternaturally warm skin. His internal temperature ran higher than a human's.

A minute detail the manuscript had gotten right.

There was a slight rap at the door to his office, and then it opened. "My apologies for my delay, sir. You requested my presence."

Lacing his fingers together behind his back, Vincent tracked the movements of the people he could see trekking through the snow-covered sidewalk below, likely in search of Christmas gifts. If he were human, the insignificant creatures going on about their insignificant lives would look like nothing more than black dots.

But he wasn't human. And the author behind the manuscript on his desk knew it.

It was against the rules to find out who authored a story, but he needed them broken. His life was more important than the rules. Vincent glanced over his shoulder. "Yes, I did. Louis, close the door."

"Yes, sir." His assistant shut the door, stepped further into the office, and swallowed. He fidgeted with the pen and pad of paper in his hands. "Have I done something wrong?"

Vincent raised an eyebrow. What nonsense were fools in the office filling his assistant's head with now? Louis was the one person he trusted in this godforsaken building. Hell, in this city. Frowning, he faced him and crossed his arms. "Of course, not. I simply need you to do something."

"Oh, of course, sir. Whatever you need." Releasing a deep breath, Louis closed some of the distance between them, stopping to collect the pens on the floor and return them and the holder to the desk.

"Leave them." Vincent snarled. He'd deal with the pens later. Once his assistant dropped the items, Vincent shifted his gaze toward the manuscript blatantly sitting on his desk. "I need you to… discreetly… find someone. And it's imperative you do it without question. Do you understand?"

Louis tilted his head. He glanced from Vincent to the manuscript on the desk and back again. "Oh! Um, yes, sir. Of course. As you wish."

"Thank you."

With a bow of his head, Louis fetched the manuscript from the large cherry desk and paused halfway to the door. He looked back at Vincent. "Sir, this is—"

"Without question."

"But sir—"

"Just do it," Vincent growled.

Louis gasped and scampered out of the office.

Vincent turned toward the window once again. His reflection stared back at him. Electricity pulsated behind his blue eyes. His jawline shifted. Even his canines elongated a touch. The monster started clawing its way out. Something he couldn't allow to happen.

Grace swept her caramel-brown hair into a ponytail and eyed the heap of books on the rolling cart. Grabbing the first one, she shifted her gaze to the wall of neatly stacked compositions. None of the novels were technically new, although many of them were new to her father's antique store. Scanning the many titles, she searched for the other Mark Twain novel they'd recently purchased.

Her love of the written word made this section of the store her favorite. Although she attended school for social work, writing helped get the visions out of her head.

Sometimes.

If she were lucky, it would help pay for school too, at least *if* the story she'd entered the local writing contest won the grand prize. She hadn't planned to submit anything to Nouveau Publishing House, but her best friend had convinced her.

The bell rang as the door opened, and a patron entered the store. She glanced over her shoulder and her gaze landed on Jagger's six-foot frame. Good God, *he* was back. She rolled her eyes and returned her attention to the shelves on the back wall. Maybe if she ignored him, he'd go away.

"Grace, you're here."

She cringed. No such luck. "Where else would I be?" Dealing with him was a nightmare; not that he'd ever given her much of a choice. He waited for her anytime she wasn't here. It had become tiresome over the last couple of months.

A set of heavy footsteps approached her from behind. "It is a big city. You could be at several places when you're not here."

Really? Since when? Her life had always been simple. Even if she hadn't been unique, she'd never gone much of anywhere or done much of anything. Practically everyone knew where to find her: the store, school, or home.

Then again, she'd always kept their conversations professional. No matter how many times he attempted otherwise. Grace spun on her heel and faced him. "What do you want?"

"I need your help to locate a book for my friend." He flashed a pearly white smile at her and brushed a hand through his jet-black hair.

Raising an eyebrow, she crossed her arms. Sure, that was exactly what he wanted. "What does your friend like?"

"You both have similar tastes. What would you recommend?"

They both knew he had no intention of buying a book. The man rarely purchased anything. "If you're here to ask me out again, the answer is still no."

"Yes, but you've never explained why. We'd be so good together."

She wasn't attracted to him. Not in the least bit. Even if she had been, her secret stopped her from dating anyone. Every relationship had ended badly because of it. "I don't see you that way."

"How would you know when you haven't given us a chance?"

"There is no us and there never will be. If you're not here to buy anything, then please go." She pointed to the door.

He scanned the store, then grabbed her arm and dragged her over to the nearby mirrors. "Come on, look at the two of us. We're both too beautiful not to go out on at least one date together."

Grace narrowed her eyes and yanked her arm from Jagger's grip. "You have to the count to three to leave before I call the cops."

"Fine," he snapped. "I'll go, but don't think for one second this is the last you've seen of me."

Vincent stopped and lifted his eyes to the sign above the door. It read *Olde Time Trinkets.* This was the address his assistant had given him. According to Louis, the author of the manuscript was a young woman named Grace Reddington who worked at her father's antique store.

He opened the door. The bell rang and tickled his ears as he stepped inside the building.

"I'll be with you in a just a minute," an angelic voice trilled out from somewhere in the back.

"Don't rush on my behalf." His words dripped with sarcasm. Vincent glanced around. To his left, there was a beautifully decorated Christmas tree nearly as tall as him next to a counter with a single large register that looked to be a bit of a relic. To his right stood two natural wood China hutches side by side. One held several teapots with matching teacups and various jewelry boxes, some made of wood and others sterling silver. The other had porcelain dolls, decorative plates, and more.

Stepping in further, he eyed the closest aisle of items. On one side was row upon row of mythological figurines, from fairies to mermaids to a phoenix. Across from them were rows of model planes, trains, and ships. From what he'd seen, it was a quaint store with decorations scattered about. Certainly explained why she'd submitted a story to his company's contest.

"Sorry about that. I was offloading some of our new products. What can I help you with?"

Her voice was even more singsong than it had been the first time he'd heard it. It fit her well.

Folding his hands together behind his back, Vincent drank her in from head to toe. She was gorgeous. A full head of light-brown hair swept away from her soft face. She had on a pair of hip-hugging skinny jeans that shaped her hourglass figure and a light blue polo shirt. "A patron should never be made to wait."

"My apologies. What can I do for you?"

"I'm here for you."

"Well, whatever you're looking for, I can help you find it, Mister ...?"

"Vincent." He practically spat his first name out. She didn't need to know anything beyond that. Narrowing his eyes, he caught a whiff of honey and a hint of an orange grove with a buttery vanilla finish. It was almost as if he had entered a bakery filled with cookies, cakes, and other trays of baked goods. The wondrous scent filling his nostrils—it belonged to her.

Leaning in, he studied her more. Her champagne-brown eyes lit up the room. It reminded him of home... before the death of his parents. No. He couldn't let her scent or beauty take him back to the depths of his past. He stared at the China hutch until the sensations coursing through his veins disappeared.

Regaining control, he steeled his eyes on the woman once again. Maybe she wasn't the one he was looking for. His assistant hadn't provided him with a photograph; it would be pertinent he confirmed the woman's identity. "And you are?"

With a slightly slackened jaw, she blatantly eyed him from his mussed hair, jaw, shoulders, and all the way to the shoes on his feet.

The corners of his lips curled. Normally it bothered him when his clients or coworkers ogled him, but with this woman... it was different. He liked the way she looked at him. Not to mention her eyes sparkled as her gaze fell over him completely. But he didn't have time for this. Not tonight. Vincent snapped his fingers.

She blinked, then squinted her champagne-brown eyes and bit her bottom lip. "Vincent?"

He growled. A blast of heat shot through his body. His gaze fell to her rose-tinted lips. They demanded to be kissed. Forcing himself to focus on her eyes, he closed some of the space between them and offered his hand. "Let's try this again. It's just Vincent. What's your name?"

"Well, 'Just Vincent,' I'm just Grace. It's a pleasure to meet you." She placed her hand in his and a slight jolt passed between the two of them.

"I'm sure—" His hand tingled as a shock from their handshake penetrated his body and set every synapse ablaze. Vincent withdrew his hand from hers and glanced from her to his hand and back again.

What the hell had just happened between them? His entire body was on fire. His skin prickled as his inner wolf attempted to claw its way free. He had to extinguish this feeling burning his insides. But he couldn't do that with her standing so close. Backing up, he stormed out of the store.

The second he exited the door, a blast of cool air slapped him in the face, but his veins were still on fire. He had to shift. It was the only way to release the inferno consuming him from the inside out. But he couldn't do it here.

With a grimace, Vincent zeroed in on the street signs. Washington Square Park was the best option, but it was several blocks away. He snarled and ran toward a nearby alleyway, but he didn't get far before the first of his bones snapped and his jacket ripped. As his body reconstructed itself to the hefty size and shape of his wolf form, the remnants of his clothes were shredded. Letting out a slight chuff, he stretched and howled. *Glorious freedom.* He took off down the alley.

Jagger scanned the park's terrain from his perch. Still nothing. As much as he wanted to, he couldn't risk getting closer. The park itself was shapeshifter territory. Who knew how many of those fuckers he'd find if he actually scoured the place from inside? A crunching sound beside him tickled his ear. He jerked his head in his companion's direction. "Laurent!" he snapped.

The male withdrew a touch and offered him a sheepish grin as he stowed the bag of chips in his jacket's pocket. "Sorry, boss."

"This is a complete bust." Jagger stood, rising from his haunches. A shit night topped off a shit day. It seemed pointless to continue watching for something to pop up. Grunting, he dismantled his rifle.

"You alright, boss?"

"I'm fine. Bad day, that's all." Carefully, he laid the various parts of his weapon in the bag and zipped it up. The last thing he wanted was to discuss his list of failures. Not just regarding hunting, but his love life. "Grace turned me down again." The words came out before he could stop them.

"Sorry to hear that." Pushing up to his feet, Laurent flicked his gaze to Jagger. "Maybe you could tell her about this. Then she might give you a chance."

He cocked an eyebrow at his friend, scoffed, and shrugged the rifle bag over his shoulder. "You know that's against our rules. We don't share the truth until *after* things become serious. Though I haven't attempted to propose anything to her father. It might be a way in."

"Isn't *that* against the rules?" Laurent snickered. He pulled the bag of chips from his pocket and popped one into his mouth. "You're a good guy. If you're so set on her, then make your own rules. Who's going to call you out on it?"

That was a valid point. He was the only one left in his family. While the city held other hunter families, they didn't all communicate with one another. He could change the rules. Make them work for him and not against his desires. "Perhaps. Come on. Let's go—"

A wolf howl sounded not far off in the distance, cutting his words off. His attention snapped in its direction. He glanced at Laurent. "That's in the city." The corners of his mouth upturned, wiggled his brows, and bolted across the roof top. Hitting the edge, he jumped over the open alley below and landed on the next roof top with ease. Though he couldn't keep it up, it brought him closer to his target.

"Wait!" Laurent hollered and took off after him.

That wasn't something he could do. Not when he had a shapeshifter close at hand. This was what he lived for. Jagger darted for the staircase and ran down them, pausing briefly at the ground level. The noise had come from around six blocks away. Without waiting for Laurent to catch up, he raced toward the alley it had come from.

Jagger skidded to a stop at the alleyway's entrance. He unsheathed a dagger he had hooked to his belt and inched forward. Scanning his surroundings, he scrutinized every rust-pitted dumpster, dirt and grime, and ratty blanket he spotted. His gaze fell upon a pile of… fabric. His eyes narrowed as he crouched down and picked up a scrap of a suit. Or at least the remnants of one. Something or someone had shredded it.

The corner of his mouth ticked upward. That howl belonged to a shapeshifter. Taking a big whiff, he inhaled deep and cleared his throat. The combined stench of vinegar and urine assaulted his nostrils. "Damn it!" he bemoaned. "No!" This couldn't be it. Jagger pressed a piece of the material against his nose. He just needed to catch the creature's scent. Except he got nothing. He only smelled rotting garbage and some other foul odor he couldn't identify.

He'd lost the fucking trail before he'd even found it. Rising to his full height, Jagger tossed the scrap into the side pocket of his rifle bag. A few tests back home might give him the edge he needed to hunt this fucker down. His gaze flicked to Laurent as the male approached. His friend stopped just to his left, bent over, and heaved in and out, struggling to catch his breath.

Jagger peered across the alleyway. No tracks to follow or any other trace of the shifter. There wasn't anything for him here. Tonight was a bust, but tomorrow was another day. He patted his friend's shoulder. "Come on; let's go get a drink."

"Hey," Laurent started on a heavy exhale. "Isn't Grace's shop nearby?"

Tilting his head, Jagger cocked an eyebrow and glanced at the mouth of the alleyway. The male was right. It wasn't more than a couple of blocks to the west. How had he overlooked how close they were? The beast had drawn all of his attention. A mistake he wouldn't make again. He sheathed his dagger. "Yeah. We should ensure she gets home safely. Then get a drink."

CHAPTER *Two*

VINCENT STARED AT the sentences of the initial offer on his desk. The words blurred together until they were nothing but senseless black lines. Exhaling, he leaned back in his leather chair and scrubbed his face.

His mind never reacted this badly to shifting before. Yes, it had been weeks since he'd let his wolf stretch, but it was still a complete anomaly. If he didn't know better, he'd swear his brain had gotten tossed in a blender, scrambled and then put back inside his head. The entire day had been a struggle from the moment he'd crawled out of bed. Selecting a suit normally took him a few minutes, yet he'd spent nearly a half hour in his closet this morning.

He groaned and snagged the bottle of water from the ceramic coaster on his desk. Taking a swig, Vincent's eyes combed the décor in his office like it held the solution to his dilemma.

Two chocolate brown leather chairs with tufted backs and round arms sat angled on the other side of his desk. Their dark color and size complemented the rich cherry oak finish of the executive desk. A piece that included oversized crown, claw feet, and decorative scrolled moldings. And no office would be complete without a couple of perfectly selected paintings.

It had taken him years to build his reputation and get to the twelfth floor of this sky-rise building. He refused to allow some… woman derail everything he'd worked for. If he didn't stop whatever was happening, then it would all slip through his fingers.

Vincent's grip on the water bottle tightened. It didn't matter what transpired between them last night or how her touch ignited something inside of him. Whatever magic she'd conjured had to be dealt with. Especially as he couldn't stop thinking about her.

All day long, Grace tip-tapped on his brain. Her champagne-colored eyes lit up the room as if the sun shone through them. Her rosy, plump lips spouting off words in the most melodic voice. He'd bet her lips tasted like succulent honey. The curve of her hips looked as if they'd been made specifically for the grip of his hands. *Fuck!* He shouldn't be thinking about this.

Readjusting in the chair, Vincent growled and fixed his slacks. His cock throbbed against the material. Just the mere thought of her drove him crazy. He craved her like he'd desired no one else. He had to get this woman out of his head. And he knew just the thing.

With a quick glance at the time on his desktop, he realized he could still get to the store and rectify the situation. He depressed the speaker button on his telephone, called his assistant, and shut his system down.

"Yes, sir?"

"Louis, cancel the rest of my meetings for the day." He collected his cell phone and stood.

"Of course, sir."

Vincent ran a hand through his hair and nodded to himself. Last night had gone to hell. Maybe it would be best if he took a personal approach. His beast stirred at the idea. It liked it. A lot.

Sweeping the snow off her wool cap, Grace entered her father's shop and removed both the earmuffs and hat from her head. She made a couple of unexpected pit stops on her way to the store. Thankfully, she was only a few minutes late for her official shift. If she'd been later—

Grace stopped in her tracks.

Her eyes landed on the blue-eyed Herculean hovering near the aisle of vases. *What the hell? He's back?* After his quick escape last night, she didn't expect to ever see him again. But there he stood, in her father's antique store for the second time in two days.

Maybe he'd finally figured out how to speak? She snickered. Wait a second… why hadn't her father—her gaze swung around, and she caught sight of another patron. One of their regulars.

She strode to the front counter where her father sat. Shucking her backpack to the floor, Grace smiled at him and kissed his cheek. "Hi, Papa."

"Hello, my beautiful daughter."

Raising an eyebrow, she took off her coat and crossed her arms. Her father never greeted her so sweetly; not unless he wanted something. "Papa?"

Her father brushed a hand through his salt and pepper hair, then leaned in close and lowered his voice. "Get that man out of our store. He refuses to deal with anyone but you. We don't need his kind in here."

His kind? Grace eyed Vincent. He looked no different from last night. Except for his suit. The pin-striped jacket and slacks clung to him like spandex, which barely left anything to the imagination. She bit her bottom lip and studied the angle of his chiseled jaw. Her gaze traced the outline of his physique. At least what she could see from her current position. She swallowed. Maybe she should get closer.

Shaking away the tingles crawling up her arms, she turned back to her father. Nothing about his statement made sense. They dealt with businessmen all the time. Maybe not of Vincent's caliber, but she could handle whatever he threw her way. "His kind? Papa, what are you talking about?"

With a scowl, her father folded his arms across his chest and dropped his gaze to the floor. "Nothing. He's… he just refused help from anyone but you."

"If you say so, Papa. I'll take care of it." Grace sighed and shook her head.

Vincent surveyed the situation at the counter out of the corner of his eye. His kind, huh? So the old man could tell he was a shapeshifter. But how? Typically, only either other shapeshifters, kin, or hunters recognized him. If his senses told him anything, the old man was human.

Perhaps, whatever sixth sense the store owner had that allowed his heightened perception had gotten passed onto Grace. It would certainly explain why she drew his wolf out. Vincent watched from his periphery as Grace and her father's conversation continued.

"Help Mrs. Carroll first. She's looking for a Christmas present for her—" Grace's father started.

"—her granddaughter. I remember."

"I knew you would."

Grace pressed a loving kiss to her father's balding head. "I've got this, Papa. Go home."

"Absolutely not. I'm not leaving you alone with *him,*" Grace's father said.

Vincent raised an eyebrow. Did the old man have a problem with shapeshifters or just him? *If* it was shapeshifters, then the man could get on board the hate train. Hunters tracked his kind down as they considered shapeshifters' abominations. Most shapeshifters patrolled nightly to get to the hunters first.

He swung his gaze back to the vases on the shelf. His focus wasn't on what was in front of him; instead, he listened intently as Grace pushed back against her father.

If he didn't know any better, he'd swear she *wanted* to be alone with him. Had she felt the jolt from last night as much as he had? No, surely that wasn't the case. Could it be?

"Papa, I'll be fine." Grace frowned.

"I can't be sure of that. Not with him around."

"Papa, the weather is getting worse outside, and I'd like to know you're at home, safe before it gets too bad."

"Stop treating me like some frail old man. I'm not going anywhere until *he* leaves."

"Fine." Grace threw her hands up in the air. With a smirk, she shoved her coat and backpack beneath the counter.

Damn, she's feisty. This was going to be fun. The corners of his mouth upturned. Vincent leveled his gaze at the various vases on the top shelf.

Turning away from her father, Grace left the front counter and passed the grandfather clocks. She continued through the mirrors and located Mrs. Carroll in the hats. Narrowing her eyes at her customer, she scrutinized the woman. "I know you're here for your granddaughter, but if you need a new hat, I have the perfect choice. We just got it in the other day."

"Oh? I mean, I am here for Alicia, but I love a good hat."

Of course, you do. She knew exactly what the woman wanted, otherwise, she wouldn't have ordered the item when she'd come across it two weeks ago. "Come with me."

The two women walked down a couple of aisles. Grace stopped and lifted a bright purple velvet fedora from the 1940s with a long white feather strapped in place by a white silk ribbon. She held the hat out to the customer, whose jaw slackened as her eyes bulged.

"How beautiful!" Mrs. Carroll exclaimed. "You're right. It's like someone made it just for me."

"My thoughts exactly, but that doesn't mean I forgot about Alicia." As much as she hated the random images that popped into her head, they helped a little with her father's store over the years. It was part of the reason she knew most of their customers on a first name basis. Most of them sought her gift recommendations.

Which was exactly what had led her to the item she procured for Mrs. Carroll's granddaughter. Grace pivoted toward the other side of the aisle. She wrapped her hands around what looked like nothing more than a yellow egg inlaid with Austrian crystals. Flipping the fastener, she opened the egg and revealed a miniature tea party inside.

Grace wound up the box. The tea party went around in circles as music played. The base of the party continued round and round and round, spinning faster and faster. At first, she only heard the woman's voice in her head.

"You bastard! Do you think I can be bought?"

A lamp flew across the living room, past the grand piano, and smashed into the pit of the fireplace. The flames burst forward and licked at the air, angry and hungry for more.

"A cold-hearted shrew can't be bought! Nothing's ever good enough for her!" The raven-haired man smirked, waved his hands at her dismissively, and walked away.

The blonde woman screamed and threw the yellow egg toward his head. It missed his ear by an inch and landed in the heart of the fire. Flames engulfed the music box. "You're a piece of shit! I hope you die!"

"Are you insane?" He ran across the room and attempted to retrieve the egg from the fire.

"No. I'm the most clear-headed I've been in years. You're the idiot who cheated on his wife. But you know what, you deserve that gold-digging whore. Not that there's going to be anything left after I'm through with you." Her red heels clicked against the marble floor as she stomped to the golden chaise across from the fireplace.

He launched over the chaise and tackled her to the ground. His green eyes narrowed, and his nostrils flared as his hands wrapped around her neck.

The yellow egg rolled out of the fireplace along the marble floor. Its latch loosened and the egg opened. Slightly charred from the fire, the tea party slowly went around in circles as the music played.

"However did you find it, my dear?" Mrs. Carroll grinned.

Grace blinked. She glanced from one side of the aisle to the other. The yellow egg was no longer in her hands. That explained part of it. If only she understood what had brought on the other part.

The part she hated.

That she wished didn't exist.

The part she—what had Mrs. Carroll asked? Oh, right. "Um, right place, right time."

"I'm thinking it's that excellent intuition of yours. It's always spot-on."

"Yeah, I guess." Whatever it was, she didn't really want to talk about it, or think about it, to be honest. She just wanted to be normal.

Normal…

That shouldn't be too much to ask for, at least not in this lifetime.

Or any lifetime.

"Well, this is absolutely perfect. My granddaughter will love it."

"I'm happy to hear that. If you take it up front, my father will check you out." Grace smiled with a small nod. She watched the woman walk away, then took a moment to collect herself. A glance over her shoulder told her Vincent still lingered in the same aisle he'd been in when she first arrived.

The hairs on the nape of Vincent's neck prickled. One corner of his mouth lifted. "Good afternoon, Grace."

"Afternoon, Just Vincent. I take it you've decided on something to purchase?"

Raising an eyebrow, he pivoted in her direction. Her eyes met his. He noticed a slight twinkle in those champagne-colored orbs. Gorgeous. "As I said last night, I'm here for you."

"While I appreciate the sentiment, I'm not for sale. Now, if there's something else in the store that interests you, then I can help." She gestured toward the multitude of aisles that occupied the store's space.

Vincent frowned. For sale? What the hell would make her think he wanted to buy her? He laced his fingers together behind his back. "Let me make something *very* clear. I'm not here to purchase you. I'm here to confirm what time your shift ends, as I'll be taking you to dinner later."

He already had it all planned out. Although he had to make a few minor adjustments to make sure it all went smoothly. He'd even considered her hours.

After all, it was obvious she closed the shop while her father opened it. In fact, he had seen no one else come in during the time he'd been here.

Taken aback, Grace blinked. Dinner? With him? She knew nothing other than his name. And gathering that much information had been like walking through a snowstorm. Drawing her breath in, she released it before opening her mouth. "It doesn't matter what time I get off. I'm not going anywhere with you."

His suit accentuated the taut lines of his powerful build. Long lashes swept over his electric blue eyes. Vincent leaned in close and lowered his voice. "Yes, you will, Grace."

Her name left his mouth in a husky whisper. The matter-of-fact way he spoke shot a blast of heat straight to her core. Tucking a loose strand of her hair behind her ear, she bit her bottom lip. If she allowed herself, she'd get lost in those blue pools of his, but she couldn't.

Glancing at the delicate swirls of a nearby vase, she inhaled and exhaled a deep breath. Her heart thundered inside her chest. The quickening of her pulse had to ease before she could appropriately address his statement.

She didn't date.

Plain and simple.

Although their handshake hadn't shown her anything, it was just a matter of time before her senses lit up like the night sky. It happened in all her past relationships. After the last one had blown up, she decided the risk was too great. Meeting new people seemed pointless, not when she knew how it would end.

And Vincent affected her more than anyone she'd ever crossed paths with before. No matter how much he set her body on fire, nothing could ever happen between them.

Looking back to him, Grace jutted her chin and met his gaze head-on. "Hear me loud and clear, Vincent. We'll never go anywhere together. *I'm* off-limits. Now, leave."

A low rumble escaped his throat. His blue eyes radiated before he closed the little distance there was between them. "You don't know this yet, but you're not off-limits to me."

His rich, woodsy cologne tantalized her nose and threatened to weaken her resolve. They were so close she could feel the heat rolling off his body. Steeling herself, Grace clenched her hands and swallowed. "You need to leave. Now."

He leaned in and whispered in her ear, "I'll go, but I will be back."

Then Vincent straightened to his full height of six-foot-six, tugged at the cuffs of his jacket, and brushed past her on his way toward the front door.

Turning off the light switch, Grace left the storage room. She surveyed the store as she strode toward the front. Back lights off—check. Christmas tree and lights unplugged—check. Aisles clutter-free—check. Cash counted and set for deposit, credit card receipts reviewed, and both locked in the office safe—all check. With everything finished for the night, she could lock up and head home.

Grace stopped at the front counter, collected her coat and shrugged it on. She'd taken her purse and backpack upstairs earlier. There'd never been a need to keep them in the shop when she lived so close. She bet that had been intentional.

Keys in hand, she flipped off the front lights and exited the store. What the fuck? Vincent stood a few feet away. Her hardened gaze met his. He had a lot of nerve showing up like this. Grace turned around and shut the heavy oak door. "What are you doing here?"

"I'm here to take you to dinner."

Hell no. He didn't just say that. She spun in his direction and narrowed her eyes. "Excuse me?"

Vincent raised an eyebrow. "I'm positive you heard what I said."

"And yet *I'm* positive you heard me when I declined your offer. Should I have said 'no, thank you'? Would that have made its way to your brain?" She just wanted to get the shop closed so she could go home. Both homework and a nice microwavable dinner awaited her, but there he stood, delaying the inevitable. Grace ground her jaw and returned her attention to the door.

Self-assured jerk couldn't possibly think she'd agree to dinner out. Fumbling with the door's lock, she twisted the key to the left. Apparently, everything had to be hard tonight. Backing up, Grace stretched on her tiptoes for the rolling steel door.

"Here, let me help." Vincent reached over her head and pulled it down.

He had a good foot on her. Their height difference offered him a better vantage point. It also put him closer to her backside than she liked. The heat from his body radiated and flooded her with warmth. The hairs on the nape of her neck rose.

Grace swallowed. Refusing to be distracted by him, she finished locking the store, exhaled a deep breath, and faced him. She smirked and dismissed him with a single nod. "Thank you."

A smile played on the corner of his mouth as he stared at her.

Her heart thundered beneath her chest. She had to get away from him. Her place was just around the corner. Taking a step forward, she brushed by him and didn't stop when a deep growl passed his lips. A blast of heat shot through her body. She hooked a left and headed toward her place.

"Where are you going?"

"Home." Hadn't she already made that clear? Lifting her chin, she continued a straight-backed stride down the sidewalk. Not much further now.

"No way in hell you're walking in this weather."

That's cute. Like he could stop her. Throwing her head back, Grace laughed, but continued forward. It had been the one benefit of living right above the store. Nevermind that her father believed it was the safest place for her, probably why he'd chosen it.

Vincent growled again. His feet pounded against the pavement as he jogged after her. Upon approaching, he slowed his pace and strolled alongside her. "If you insist on walking, I'm going to accompany you home."

"Okay." Oh, he could insist all he wanted. It wouldn't get him far. Beaming, she stopped in front of a staircase not over thirty feet from the front door of the antique store. It was set at the corner of the building *Olde Time Trinkets* occupied.

It had been a couple of years since she moved in; the year she'd spent searching for a place of her own had been worth it. She got her privacy, and her father kept her protected. Win-win for everyone.

Swallowing, Vincent rubbed his eyebrow and his gaze met hers.

The blue in his eyes sparkled. He had to stop looking at her like that. Tingles ran down the back of her spine. It made it difficult for her to keep pushing him away. No matter how her body responded, it was the right thing to do.

Yeah, she could take him upstairs to her apartment, remove the pin-striped suit piece by piece, and explore every part of his muscular body. Fire coursed through her veins. A slight flush of her skin warmed her cheeks and neck. She couldn't act out her fantasies about him; it would open up a can she'd never be able to close.

Clenching his hands into fists, Vincent opened his mouth and snapped it shut. Her radiant smile sent a bolt of heat surging through his body.

Nothing about any of this made sense. From how far they hadn't gone to his need to chase after her.

Unless—that couldn't be possible. Not after the way he'd destroyed his pack. No way he deserved—

A mate? His mate? Maybe he couldn't stop himself from chasing after her, but it certainly wasn't because she was his destined mate. He'd accepted a long time ago it wasn't in the cards. His wolf would forever remain alone.

"I'm home." Grace tilted her head toward the staircase.

Right. His assistant had mentioned her home address was somewhere near the shop. It just hadn't registered it would be *this* close. "You live above the store?"

"Yes." With no further explanation, Grace pivoted on the ball of her foot and started up the stairs.

Nothing had gone according to his plan, but he refused to let it end there. Vincent followed her.

Stopping halfway up, she faced him. "What are you doing?"

"Seeing you home."

With a sigh, she pinched the bridge of her nose. "What will it take for you to go away?"

"Give me your phone." He held out his hand. It was a last-ditch effort, but it was the only option he had left.

Grace's eyes narrowed as she crossed her arms over her chest, staring at him for a minute. With a groan, she handed him the cell phone from her coat pocket. "Just don't run off with it."

"I'm not a thief." Vincent frowned. He typed in the nickname she'd given him the night before and his private phone number, shot himself a quick text, and then returned it to her. "Saturday, eight o'clock. And I won't take no for an answer."

He flashed another smile and descended the staircase. This time, she would join him for dinner. No questions asked.

"Wait, what? No," Grace said. "Vincent! Vincent!"

Ignoring her response, he continued across the street and climbed in the black Lincoln as if he hadn't heard a word. Not even when she called his name.

Propping his elbow on the driver's side window, he sat in the car and stared at her standing in the middle of the staircase. She spun on her heel and stormed up the stairs to her apartment. Her brows pinched together as she shoved the key into the lock and threw open the door.

Vincent started the vehicle and his cell phone dinged. The incoming message flashed across the car's display.

I'll consider dinner on Saturday, but you have to tell me why

you're so confident I'll go.

With a grin, he dug his phone out of his inner pocket. He could give her several reasons, but only one mattered. And it was the most honest answer he could give her, too. Vincent tapped his response and hit send.

Your curiosity will win out over your determination.

CHAPTER *Three*

"WHAT HAPPENED TO you last night?" Chip asked.

"What're you talking about?" Grace took a big bite of the BBQ Bacon burger in her hands. Last night had been strange. Nothing about her life was normal, but Vincent showing up after only two conversations—for a date—went beyond the usual level of weird.

It had been one reason she'd been grateful for lunch with Chip today. It may have been part of their weekly ritual, but she needed his thoughts about her encounters with Vincent. Yeah, she'd said she was "off limits," but when he looked at her, even spoke to her, her words had next to no conviction.

Swallowing the bite of leafy greens in his mouth, Chip raised an eyebrow. "You didn't call or text me back at all. You just disappeared after you got off work."

Shit. Chip *had* texted her last night, hadn't he? Grace popped a fry in her mouth to avoid an immediate answer. Her brain had been in such a haze after her encounter with Vincent, she hadn't thought about anything else. The way his electrifying blue eyes caressed her body. Or how the suit he'd worn had been flawless in its fit, clinging to him like grass burrs to jeans.

A shiver crept up the back of her spine. She had to stop thinking about him.

"Hello? Earth to Grace."

Grace took a sip of juice to wet her parched throat and sighed. "I'm sorry. I didn't mean to zone out."

"Where'd you go just now?"

"I was thinking about why I didn't hit you back last night." It was the truest statement possible. She'd never intentionally lie to her best friend. Unless hiding her ability from him counted, but she hated talking about that with anyone. Mostly, she preferred not to even think about it. As far as she was concerned, if she didn't think about it, then it didn't exist, and she could be…

Well, she could be normal.

"Inquiring minds want to know."

Taking another bite of the burger, Grace narrowed her eyes. How could she explain it without admitting her attraction to Vincent? Then again, that *was* the problem. He'd demanded dinner with her twice, and deep down, she wanted to go.

The corner of her lips curled into a half-smile. "I had a last-minute client show up. One that was… rather difficult."

Chip chuckled. "You mean someone got you flustered?"

"Something like that." She scowled at his amusement. It wasn't all that funny. Vincent was cocky and highly presumptuous. He may be… well, gorgeous, and charming in a know-it-all sort of way, but he was persistent, too persistent for her to keep him at bay—not that she wanted to.

Chip leaned back in a dusky rose office chair and grinned. "I see. This *client* has really gotten to you. Hasn't he?"

Squinting her eyes, she pursed her lips. Wait a second. She hadn't mentioned her *client's* gender. Chip read her too easily. Grace groaned. "Fine. Yes. He's an arrogant ass who acts like I'm going to fall at his feet."

"In other words, you met a guy who doesn't find you intimidating." Chip snickered and shook his head. "Has he asked you out?"

"Sort of." Only if she counted his demands for dinner as a question. Clenching her jaw, she folded her arms across her chest. "He didn't ask. Instead, he told me he was taking me to dinner Saturday night."

"Sounds like the kind of guy you need."

"I don't need a guy. We both know I have horrible taste in men." Her best friend knew most of the truth about her past three ex-boyfriends. And she could sum up each into four words: cheater, liar, drug-dealer. Yep, she had impeccable taste in men.

Not once had Chip inquired how she'd found out about any of her exes' issues. Especially the last one: Gabriel. She still remembered that vision as if it had just appeared in her head.

"I showed you mine. Now let me see yours," Gabriel said.

An imposing, olive-skinned man stood in front of a nearby silver sports car and closed a duffle bag. A few feet behind him sat a black SUV with tinted windows in an unmarked alleyway. Not far off, a tall man hung back by the SUV.

"You right." The man closest to Gabriel glanced over his shoulder. "Show 'em the paper."

Silent and dark eyes, the other guy opened the passenger side of the SUV and stepped back from behind the door with a black bag in his hands. He closed the distance between him and Gabriel, and then handed the bag over.

Gabriel unzipped the bag, saw a pile of cash, and beamed. "Good as gold. Holler at me when you're ready to place another order."

It was much later when she realized the dirty cash Gabriel had left on the restaurant table had triggered the vision. She had never figured out when the deal had occurred.

It had taken almost a month after that dinner to see the signs that had been there all along. He had always carried cash, never once used a bank, diverted her attention any time she asked about his job, and anytime they went anywhere, they sat in the back hidden from the cameras. Not to mention, she met none of his friends.

She had spent too long overlooking what had been in front of her face. Maybe that was the key. So, what hadn't she yet discovered about Vincent?

"You can't let the past define your future. Hasn't your past taught you to trust your instincts?"

Her experiences had taught her something all right. Not to date. That people, in general, couldn't be trusted. As for her instincts… shit, how did she argue against that? Yeah, she knew little about Vincent. He'd hidden a lot…

Even his last name. He'd inputted his name in her phone as "Just Vincent."

"Of course, it has and there are too many unknowns with this guy." Yes, her body lit up like the night sky whenever he was around. There was something about him. Something different she couldn't put her finger on… yet.

Tilting his head, Chip stroked his chin. "You said the date was on Saturday. What if I met this guy tomorrow for lunch and did an assessment for you?"

"Excuse me?" Her eyes widened as she jumped out of the chair. "I don't need you to interrogate or approve of a date of mine. I can choose my date."

"Hey, you were the one who said there were too many unknowns." He shrugged as his desk phone rang.

Grace glared daggers at Chip. Vincent dodged one question, the only question she'd asked. Her desire to know more about him hadn't spawned anymore questions. At least not ones she vocalized, though she *wanted* to know more about him. Saturday seemed like the perfect opportunity. As long as she worked everything out in her favor.

She dug her cell phone out of the back pocket of her jeans, pulled up Vincent's contact information, and shot him a quick text.

Vincent flipped through the last few pages of the initial offer he'd previously set aside. Yesterday, his brain had been an enemy and refused to cooperate with anything on his schedule.

Today, he'd flown through his work with ease. Not only had he finished all his meetings for the day, but he'd successfully moved onto everything he'd canceled the day before.

Although he hadn't heard from Grace since last night, he didn't anticipate her backing out of their date on Saturday. She desired him. He'd seen it in her champagne eyes, those full and kissable lips, and in that delectable honey scent that consumed him from the inside out.

The memory of her set his veins on fire. If he had his way, he'd show her exactly how much she—

His cell phone vibrated. Vincent glanced at his phone and his heart swelled.

It was a text message from Grace.

What should I wear Saturday night?

Louis's voice came over the intercom. "Sir, I have Mr. Descoteaux on line one for you."

With a low growl, Vincent scrubbed his face and pushed any thought of Grace from his mind. He had work to do. Exhaling a deep breath, he picked up the receiver from its cradle. "Good afternoon, Chip. How are you?"

"I'm well. And you? Are you feeling better?"

"Yes, much. I appreciate your flexibility with our meeting yesterday." Pleasantries went a long way to maintaining a good relationship with literary agents. Not just for authors, but for editors as well. In his position, he discovered he could be polite without getting personal. And he liked it that way, especially with Chip Descoteaux.

The young man hadn't been on the scene for over four years, but he had an excellent eye for sellable work and was a real shark at contract negotiations. Unlike a couple of other literary agents, Vincent enjoyed working with him. Then again, he hadn't met many literary agents who were shapeshifter kin, but that hadn't ever affected their working relationship.

"Of course. I'd much rather have you in tip-top shape when reviewing a client's manuscript or an initial offer than sludging through. That's not something that would benefit either of us."

That wasn't how he would've described it. Then again, he had reread the pages on his desk several times the day before and comprehended nothing. Maybe he had been "'sludging through.'" "Well, I met with our acquisitions committee and I have the initial offer. Do you have time now to go over it?"

"Actually, I have a client in my office right now. Could we schedule some time on Monday? Say 2PM."

"Let me check my calendar." His gaze drifted to his cell phone. Vincent picked it up and tapped out a response.

I knew you'd come around.

He shifted his attention to his desktop and accessed his schedule for the following week. He had a few meetings set for the morning, but his entire afternoon was clear. "Monday at two works for me."

"Excellent. We'll talk then."

"Sounds good." His phone vibrated again.

Just answer the question.

"Have a good day," Chip said.

"You too." Vincent returned the receiver to its cradle. He sat back with his cell in his hands. The arrangements for Saturday were still being finalized, but he knew exactly how she should dress.

Something elegant. Be ready by 7.

If they were having dinner at her place, his answer would've been much different. He'd take her to his place once he had the redecorating finished. He couldn't risk it being linked back to her manuscript.

Where are we going? I'll meet you there.

Meet him there? Hell no. Vincent frowned. That wasn't how his parents had raised him. He'd pick her up, no questions asked.

It's a surprise. I'll pick you up at 7.

Absolutely not. Just tell me where to meet you at.

A knock on his office door caught his attention. He looked up as his assistant stepped inside and shut the door. "I have your reservations made, sir."

"Perfect. Where did you make them?"

"Eleven Madison Park."

Vincent squinted and shook his head. His instructions had been simple, and Louis was no fool. There shouldn't have been any reason for the man not to follow them. "I told you to make it someplace they wouldn't know me. It has to be someplace upscale where I won't be recognized."

"Sir, no matter where I make the reservation, it must still go under your name. Your identity cannot be hidden. I implore you to reconsider your decision to take Miss Reddington out to dinner. The consequences are too great."

His heart thundered in his chest and his blood boiled. Reconsider? Out of the question. He knew the risk he was taking if anyone discovered him, not just with his career, but Louis's as well. The consequences of not seeing her far outweighed the risk. Vincent growled. "No. Now, get out. I'll take care of the reservation myself."

Louis swallowed. "But sir—"

"I said, 'get out,'" Vincent snarled, his upper and lower canines elongating as his wolf threatened to make an appearance.

Gasping, Louis's face turned ashen. He spun on his heel and nearly tripped over his feet on his way out the door.

Damn it. With a heavy sigh, Vincent scrubbed his face. He didn't mean for any part of his beast to come out, but no one would stand between him and Grace. Not even his assistant.

Bottom line, Grace belonged to him.

Grace shoved her hands in the pockets of her coat as she strode along the sidewalk. For the last month, she'd agonized over what to get her father for Christmas. The man was practically impossible to shop for. Until the other day. After the whole Vincent incident, they'd gotten in an order of books, which included his favorite author. He was a big Ed McBain fan.

Although she could've easily made the trip from the school library to The Strand Bookstore, she went with an alternative. It was only a few blocks from the university, something that also applied to Mysterious Bookshop. She thought she'd have better luck at the latter rather than the former. Not to mention the owner of the Mysterious Bookshop was a publisher of Ed McBain.

This was the time of year she loathed walking anywhere. It wasn't too far for her to make the trek. And her focus on staying warm helped keep her thoughts from Vincent and their date later this evening.

What had she been thinking, agreeing to it? It was simple. She hadn't been thinking. No, Chip had been in her ear, prattling on about how the man had gotten to her. Of course he had. He'd shown up twice to her work, blatantly brushed off her feelings, and made her feel things no one else had ever done before.

Okay. It was one date. She could handle one date. They'd meet at the restaurant, giving her the perfect opportunity to get to know him better. As long as she could keep her body in check, and the whore didn't betray her… again.

Slowing her pace, Grace eyed the storefront before she pushed open the door and stepped inside. Her gaze fell across the wall-to-wall books. The shelves almost reached to the ceiling. There were a few other shorter bookcases full of books in the middle of the store. It didn't appear to be much, but there were a lot of novels lining those shelves.

She wiped her shoes on the mat to clear off any snow and ventured further inside. Yes, she knew roughly what she was looking for, but she had to figure out their organization system first. After all, the store only carried mystery, crime fiction, espionage, and thrillers.

"Can I help you find something?" A blonde-haired female asked.

"Uh, yeah. I'm looking for books by Ed McBain… if you have any." She didn't think it would be a long shot, but best to ask, so she didn't waste time hunting all over the store. Her plan was to get home, stow the book away, and wrap it later, after she checked in with her father.

"We do. Right this way." The female smiled and gestured for her to follow.

With a small nod, she walked further into the store, letting the female lead her past a staircase with crime tape across the door. Her gaze lingered for only a moment. It was marked 'office.' She'd read something about that. Some kind of joke by the owner or something to that effect. Continuing after the blonde-haired woman, Grace stopped in front of a bookcase with a decent section of Ed McBain books. Way more than she expected. How was she ever going to choose?

"Let me know if you need anything else." The woman offered her another smile and left her to her musings.

Great. She didn't know which books he already had. Or even which ones he didn't. It had been that one book they'd gotten in that had started a conversation and given her the idea. She attempted to replay everything he'd said in her mind. Had he mentioned whether he had that book?

Chewing on her bottom lip, she scanned through the different titles. There were so many. And… he didn't have it. That's right! He wouldn't buy something from his own stock. Now, she just had to remember—her eyes paused on one book with a red dust jacket: "The Frumious Bandersnatch."

That was it! Grace carefully extracted the novel and checked the price. Wow! More than she expected it to be. She dug her cell phone out of the back pocket of her jeans and executed a quick search. Alright. The author died thirteen years ago. Certainly explained the price. And… oh, it was a signed copy.

Yeah. This was definitely one Christmas gift her father would love.

Grace ran her hands along the skirting of the cocktail dress. With its fitted waist and asymmetrical skirt, it accentuated her curves well. The natural hues of her hair complemented the burgundy color of the dress.

She smiled at her reflection in the mirror. It was a good choice. Lifting her wrist, she checked the time on her watch. Her cab should arrive shortly.

It had taken nearly an hour the other day to pry the location of the restaurant out of Vincent. He'd been—

There was a knock at her front door. *Who could that be?* The store hadn't closed yet, so it couldn't be her father. Chip promised not to pop by until tomorrow. She stepped out of her bedroom and strode down the hallway. Her heels clicked against the hardwood floor of her loft-style apartment as she walked toward the door and opened it.

Vincent stood on the other side; his dirty-blond hair perfectly coiffed. The dark suit he wore hugged his powerful build, leaving next to nothing to the imagination. His long lashes swept over his electric-blue eyes as his gaze caressed her body from head to toe. "You look beautiful."

Grace swallowed and pushed the sight of his broad shoulders and the taut lines of his muscular legs from her mind. He had no right to pull a stunt like this. Clenching her jaw, she glared at him. "This isn't what we agreed on."

Holding a single-stem red rose, his lips upturned into a mischievous grin. "I know."

"You know? Yet, you disregarded my wishes anyway. Are you out of your fucking mind?" Grace crossed her arms and ground her teeth. He had a lot of nerve. She established the rules of their date for a reason. Was it too much to expect him to respect that?

He raised an eyebrow at her. "A gentleman always picks up his date."

"And disrespects his date in the process," she scoffed and slammed the door in his face.

Thrusting his hand out, Vincent grabbed the door and stepped past the doorjamb, right into her personal space. "Oh, no you don't."

"Excuse me?" Her heart pounded. The hairs on the nape of her neck rose. He was so close, the smell of the forest rolled off him in waves. Part of her wanted to shove him out of her doorway. The other part of her wanted to pull him against her and crush her lips to his.

"You aren't getting rid of me that easily."

Get rid of him? She didn't want to do that either, but she refused to let him off the hook. Grace scowled. "Fine, then explain yourself."

"Fine, but can we talk inside?" Vincent nodded toward her living room.

Let him inside? Into her private space? She could keep him in the doorway, but then she risked her father overhearing. His initial reaction to Vincent hadn't been positive. The last thing she needed was a lecture. With a deep sigh, Grace backed up and out of the way.

"Thank you." His hand grazed hers as he strolled forward and headed further into her minimally decorated apartment.

Swallowing saliva to wet her dry throat, she watched him as he moved across the room in three long, powerful strides. He stopped halfway to the couch and spun to face her. Drawing her attention away from his perfectly round ass, her eyes lifted to his hooded gaze. Shivers crept up her spine. Grace shut the door and propped herself against it.

His lips parted, and he slowly closed the distance between them. "I'm sorry I disregarded your wishes, but I came to pick you up because I couldn't *wait* to be near you. Couldn't *wait* to see your gorgeous face. Hear your sexy voice. For your sparkling eyes to look at me." Vincent leaned in and stroked her cheek. "Is that a good enough reason?"

She bit her bottom lip and nodded.

His eyes dropped to her mouth. He growled and brushed his thumb across her bottom lip. "You've got to stop that, otherwise I may not make it through dinner without kissing you."

Grace gasped at the tingling sensation that coursed through her body.

Staring at him, she lost the last bit of control she had and licked her lips.

Fire burned in his electric-blue eyes right before his lips crushed hers in a deliciously punishing kiss, his hand wrapping around her waist as he tugged her closer.

She grabbed his arms as the kiss deepened and their tongues entangled. A blast of heat shot straight to her core, and her body shuddered beneath his touch.

Releasing the kiss, Vincent nipped at her bottom lip and caressed her cheek. "I told you to stop."

"I couldn't." Grace beamed, telling him the absolute truth. She hadn't been able to stop herself. If she had to do all over it again, she wouldn't have done it any differently. Her stomach rumbled.

He returned her smile and placed a tender kiss on her forehead. "This mean you're ready to go to dinner now?"

With a soft chuckle, she nodded. She had little in the way of Christmas decorations. What little she had around her place, she had unplugged for the night. "Yeah. I think so. I just need to grab my purse and coat."

"Why don't I get your coat while you get your purse?"

Grace opened her mouth and snapped it shut. She could get it all on her own, but if they worked together, they'd get out of here faster. She pointed to the hall closet across from the kitchen. "It's the tan one."

"I can handle that."

She left him to collect her coat while she gathered her purse from her bedroom in the back. None of this had been what she'd expected when she agreed to the date. Then again, she still knew little about him.

Tonight, that would change.

CHAPTER *four*

GRACE LIFTED HER gaze to him. "Anything catching your eye?"

A lot of things had caught his attention. The way her eyes lit after every new item they tasted. How she moaned with each bite. The way she fidgeted with the dessert menu in her hands. Setting the cardboard menu down, Vincent leaned across the table and lowered his voice. "Yes, but I don't think they serve it here."

Hugging the menu to her chest, her eyes twinkled as she bit her bottom lip. "I'm sure they don't."

"What did I …" His words trailed off. Vincent narrowed his gaze as a familiar voice made its way over the din to his ears. Damn it. It was one of his coworkers.

What the hell is Aurora doing all the way out here? He'd purposely chosen Zenkichi for a multitude of reasons. One: no one knew him here. Two: no one from his office ever traveled across the bridge. Three: he and Grace had a semi-private table.

His coworker's arrival forced him to change course. He depressed the button at their table and called the server over.

"Have we decided on a dessert?" their server asked.

Removing his wallet from the inside of his jacket, he shifted his gaze to the young woman. "We've decided to skip dessert. Can we have our check, please?"

With a warm grin, the server nodded and set a black book on the table. "I'll take that—"

"Here." He didn't bother to look at the check. Vincent placed a credit card inside the book and handed it back to her.

"I'll be back momentarily." The young woman bowed her head and left the table.

"Care to explain?"

Dessert had gone out the window; at least here it had. Their only option was to leave. Vincent sifted through the noise until he located Aurora. He needed to know where they'd sat her before he answered Grace's question.

He heard her voice about five booths up on the opposite side of the aisle. It meant they'd have to go over one aisle to the left to get to the front door unseen.

Keeping a tab on his coworker, he returned his attention to Grace. Her lips pressed into a white slash, her arms folded across her chest emphasizing the peekaboo cut in the front of her dress. Even angry, she was beautiful. Vincent canted his head and offered her a small smile. "There's a pastry shop close to here that has better dessert options."

"Then why didn't you say anything earlier?"

"Because I just thought about it."

Their server chose that moment to return with the billfold. He took his credit card from the folder and shoved it in his pocket. Adding a decent-sized tip, he signed the check and closed the book. "Shall we?"

"Sure."

Vincent stood and helped Grace to her feet. He glanced down the aisle just as Aurora slipped out of the booth she'd taken and headed in their direction.

Shit. No time to get their coats on. Grabbing their coats from the booth, he grasped Grace's hand and rushed toward the end of the aisle. They'd barely rounded the corner when Aurora passed the booth he and Grace had occupied.

He peered over his shoulder and urged Grace along until they reached the front door. Leading her outside, Vincent looked back one last time. It appeared they had escaped unseen.

Grace yanked her hand from his grip. "Give me my coat."

"Here." He held it out.

Glaring, she jerked it right out of his hands. Shoving her bare arms into the sleeves, she stormed off toward the sidewalk.

Tugging his own coat on, he followed her. "Where are you going?"

"Home," she snapped.

Damn it. Vincent growled. Despite their earlier issue, the night had gone well. Now it seemed they were right back where they'd started. "You sure as hell aren't walking there."

It may not have been snowing like last time, but snow still covered the ground and it was cold. She also wasn't around the corner from home either. Yet she continued forward.

There was no way in hell they were doing this tonight. He jogged ahead, stopped in front of her, and gripped her arms. "This is no time to be stubborn. If you want to go home, I'll take you home."

"You think I'm being stubborn? Screw you!" Grace wrenched her arms from his hold and glowered at him. Flames blazed in those champagne eyes of hers. Heat rolled off her, and it was hot enough to melt the surrounding snow.

Her scent intensified. It was almost like he'd buried his nose is a pot of honey. The glow from her stare sparked an inferno in his groin. Fuck. Vincent leaned in close, slid a hand around her waist, and tossed her over his shoulder.

"Put me down!" Grace pounded on his back with her fists. "I'm not a rag-doll to be manhandled."

Vincent smirked. Oh, she was no rag-doll. The warmth of her body, the scorch of her stare… she may be his undoing, but definitely not a rag-doll.

He strode across the street to the parking garage where they'd left his car. "Are you going to take off again?"

"Yes!"

"Then no. Not until you calm down and promise to behave." He could think of much better ways to have her close to him. They all started with another kiss and ended with her naked underneath him.

"Calm down? You feed me some bullshit line about a dessert shop, practically drag me out of the restaurant into the freezing cold and you expect me to calm down! You're out of your fucking mind if you think I'm going to calm down anytime in the immediate future."

Shit. As careful as he'd been with their strategic exit, he hadn't factored in Grace's reaction. Their bodies responded differently to the cold air. He'd been so focused on getting them out of there that he'd forgotten she was human.

Vincent stepped onto the sidewalk outside the parking garage and eased Grace from his shoulder. Holding onto her waist, he ensured her feet were steady on the ground. "You're right. I'm sorry."

She raised an eyebrow and jutted her chin. "I want to believe you mean that, but this has just been tacked onto your inability to answer direct questions."

Sidestepping her questions hadn't just been about his protection, it had been a way to protect her, too. Not that he could say that. He'd determined over the last couple of hours she knew nothing about shapeshifters.

There had to be a way to give her information without causing harm to either of them. The corners of his lips upturned. "How about we start over? There really is a pastry shop near to here and I promise to answer all of your questions."

With her hands still on his arms, Grace tilted her head and peered up at him. "Tell me your last name and I'll consider it."

"LeBlanc." The name tumbled out of his mouth before he stopped it.

"Like the actor?"

"Yes, but there's no relation." Vincent caressed her cheek. "Now, how about we get some dessert?"

She leaned into his touch and let out a soft sigh. "You're a real smooth cat. I'll give you that." The corner of her mouth lifted. "Dessert sounds good."

Wolf, but she wouldn't get the correction. He offered her his arm. "Then let's go get something sweet. Or semi-sweet, if that's your preference." Otherwise, he might just throw her over his shoulder, carry her to the car, and… Wow! Where had *that* desire come from?

Grace raised an eyebrow and curled her fingers around his biceps. "Where did your mind just go?"

It seemed like an out-of-nowhere question. Nothing he'd seen of her gave him the impression she was telepathic. Or had magic or special abilities of any kind. His brows furrowed as he led them toward the pastry shop. "What makes you think it went somewhere?"

"I'm very good at reading facial expressions." She cracked a grin. "There was a glint in your eyes and then you averted your gaze."

Vincent let out a wry chuckle. *Damn, she's good.* He shoved one hand in his pocket and dipped his chin, acknowledging her statement. "How much I enjoyed holding you."

Her cheeks flushed pink and her champagne eyes sparkled. "Don't let that earlier kiss give you any ideas. We're so not there."

Although she didn't include the word, he heard the implied *yet.* He leaned down and whispered, "Your tone says otherwise." He sensed the shiver that shot down her spine. Her honey scent intensified in his nostrils. A blast of heat went straight to his cock. Fuck, he really needed to behave. At this rate, their bodies would override any sensibility they had to her declaration.

"Perhaps, but I believe it's just a case of mind over matter."

Stopping in front of the pastry shop, he busted out in laughter. How could he argue with that logic? "Touché." Vincent gripped the door handle and held it open for her. He watched as she slipped inside, brushing against him. Mmm. Getting there might just be torture, but he'd enjoy every second.

Grace tilted her head and raised an eyebrow. "You know, this isn't exactly what I had in mind when you said brunch." Eating together inside Vincent's car, parked across the street from her apartment, didn't equal an actual date. Though he had come with almost a four-course meal, she thought he'd intended to take her somewhere.

He narrowed his piercing blue eyes at her. "I'd happily carry all of this food upstairs to your place."

"And let you invade my space? Not happening." She didn't trust herself enough to keep her hands to herself. Not when he looked so damn delectable in his three-piece suit. It hugged his chiseled body perfectly. Even from this angle. Seriously, did this man wake up looking like a god? Adjusting in the leather seat, Grace bit her lower lip. Fuck, she had to stop staring at him.

Vincent let out a low growl, reached across the center console, and curled his fingers around the back of her neck. "What have I told you about doing that?"

A shiver shot down her spine. The sounds he made and the huskiness in his voice shouldn't do things to her, but they did. It set her body on fire. She closed the distance between them and lazily ran her fingers up his arm. "Maybe I can't help myself."

"Find a way," he demanded, with a rumble rising from deep within his chest.

Shit. She could practically feel the vibration through every synapse. That just made her *want* to do it more. "What if I can't?"

He leaned in and whispered in her ear, "Then I'm going to take you out of this car, throw you over my shoulder, carry you up those stairs, and… well, let's just say we'll melt the snow."

Grace jerked back. "I seriously hope you're joking." Hadn't they addressed that caveman shit last night? She hadn't cared for it then and certainly didn't want it now. Even if the rest of his declaration sent a blast of heat straight to her core. A cold shower could fix that mess.

Flashing her a toothy grin, he dipped his chin toward her vegetable frittata. "Finish up. We still have another course to go."

With a slight shake of her head, she sat back in her seat. "I don't even know where you expect me to put any more food." The fruit bowl and scone had nearly filled her up. She'd only gotten through about half of this dish, which saddened her a bit. It smelled divine. The sweet and earthy scent of mushrooms mixed with a hint of caramelized onion assaulted her nostrils. Stuffed or not, she'd eat every bite. Grace shoved another forkful in her mouth.

"I just want to ensure you enjoy everything I selected and that you have all the energy required for the day."

"Exactly how much do you expect me to burn?" The first course would've gotten her through until dinner. With maybe a tiny snack in between.

"Whatever you don't burn at work, I'll help you address… tonight." The corner of his mouth curled as he popped a bite of frittata into his mouth.

The forkful of egg stopped halfway to her mouth. A jolt of lightning lit up her synapses, setting that juncture between her thighs on fire. Fuck. Some small part of her wanted to let him have his way, but she refused to cave into those desires. "Oh? Are you planning another date for us? What makes you think I'll agree?"

"My charm has convinced you to join me for two. A third only seems the natural course."

"Your arrogance never ceases to wonder." With a slight snicker, she finished the last of her frittata.

"Confidence," he corrected. Vincent collected her empty container, placed it atop his, and returned it and their forks to the wicker picnic basket. He retrieved two spoons and two small metal bowls, removed the covers, and frowned.

"What's wrong?" She glanced at the soupy concoction inside the bowls.

"It melted."

Barely stifling a chuckle, Grace covered her mouth with her fingers. A look of annoyance crossed his face. "I'm sorry. I shouldn't laugh, but maybe this is a sign that a four-course brunch is too much."

His eyebrows drew tightly together. "Perhaps."

She got the sense that didn't quite satisfy him. That didn't mean she couldn't come up with a compromise. Time wasn't on their side at the moment. "I need to get to work. So, why don't you walk me back to my place and we'll just say you owe me dessert?"

Locking the covers on the containers, he returned them to the basket. His blue eyes sparkled as he smirked. "That sounds amenable."

The glimmer alone told her all she needed to know, but she refused to question the ideas tumbling around his brain. Not right now, anyway. Grace gripped the door handle. "Then let's go."

"Wait there." Vincent shut off the ignition and climbed out of the vehicle before she objected. He strode around the car, opened the passenger side door, and held out his hand.

None of this seemed necessary, but it seemed unreasonable to deny him now. Laying her hand in his, palm to palm, she accepted his help, and got out of the car. Together, they strolled across the semi-busy street and ascended the staircase to her apartment. "Should I expect you at any particular time tonight?"

"Closing time sounds appropriate. I rather enjoyed that the other night."

Of course he did. They stopped in front of her door. She faced him. Grabbing a hold of his button-up, Grace locked her gaze on Vincent and bit her bottom lip.

His glossy blue eyes fell from her gaze to her lips as he braced his hands on either side of her body against the door of her apartment. He dipped his head close to her face. "You're teasing me."

"Maybe." She grinned. It was his own fault. He was the one who'd admitted what it did to him. Who was she not to take advantage of that knowledge? Especially after all that had happened between them.

"If you plan to get the store open, I suggest you stop."

Grace chuckled and shook her head. She had to open the store. They did their best business during Christmas. "Then I'd have to explain the loss of money to my father."

"Well, we certainly don't want that." Cupping her cheek, he brushed a soft kiss across her lips.

The feeling of his lips warmed her body. Beaming, she unlocked her apartment. "I'll see you later."

"Count on it." Vincent kissed her one last time before heading downstairs toward the road.

She stood there for a moment and ogled him. The slacks he'd opted to wear for brunch hugged his nice, round ass like a second skin. Grace shivered as goosebumps crawled all over her body.

Looking away, she stepped into her apartment and shut the door. The last twenty-four hours between them had been intense. As much as she enjoyed brunch this morning, she was grateful for work today. It would give her time to weigh everything that had occurred.

She'd laid out her work attire earlier. She headed down the hallway to her bedroom and changed out of her dressier jeans into a grungier pair.

There was a brief knock at her front door, and then it opened. "Grace?"

What the hell? She poked her head out of her bedroom. "Chip? What're you doing here?"

"I came by to see how your date went last night. Now I'm trying to figure out why I just saw you kissing Vincent Pelissier."

No, that wasn't—he had to be joking. The grimace on Chip's face told her otherwise. Her body froze. It couldn't be true. No way had she kissed an editor of Nouveau Publishing House. Grace shook her head. "No, you're mistaken. His name's Vincent LeBlanc."

"I've worked with this man; I know what he looks like. Are you trying to ruin your chances of winning this contest?" Frowning, his brow wrinkled.

This isn't happening. She sagged against the doorway to her bedroom. Again, she put herself out there. Again, she gave someone a chance, and he lied. Everything was supposed to be different this time. Tears prickled the corners of her eyes.

Grace shifted her gaze to Chip. Did he seriously ask her that? "Of course not! I didn't know that was his name. He didn't tell me."

"How could you not know? Didn't you check the website?"

"Yes, but he doesn't have a picture, and by his name, it just says 'V. Pelissier.' If I had known that, I sure as hell wouldn't have gone out with him." The date she deserved. That began with a toe-curling—nope, she wouldn't go there.

She pushed off the doorjamb and strode into the kitchen. Checking the time on the microwave, she reached into the cabinet above it and pulled out a bottle of vodka.

"That's who you went out with last night. Seriously?"

Briefly nodding, Grace poured herself a shot and knocked it back. She winced as the clear liquid burned down the back of her throat.

"For fuck's sake, he's one of the judges."

"You're the one who told me to go. You even helped me pick out a dress." This was bad, terrible.

"If you'd told me that's who your date was with, I wouldn't have encouraged you."

She paused with the second shot halfway to her mouth and glanced at Chip. "He's one of the judges?"

"Yes!"

Vincent had to have known about her entry. It all made sense. Never once offered his full name. Playing dodgeball with her questions. Dragging her out of the restaurant last night like a stolen toy. Eating brunch this morning in his car instead of an actual restaurant.

Eyeing the clock one more time, she knocked the shot in her hand back and returned the vodka to its rightful place. There wasn't sufficient time to aptly handle the situation. The store opened in thirty minutes.

Grace spun on the back of her heel and walked to her bedroom. She plucked her cell phone off the sky-blue comforter on her bed. There was a text message—from Vincent.

Looking forward to seeing you again. Soon.

She should have responded, but she had work to do. Instead, Grace shut off her phone and tucked it into the back pocket of her jeans.

"What're you doing? We need to get a handle on this PR nightmare."

"I'm getting ready for work." Ever the vigilant literary agent; Chip worked with publicists who dealt with stupid shit like this regularly. Not that he'd convinced her they were there… yet.

"Grace, we need—"

"To do nothing. You'll let me handle it. End of story." Chip may have helped her with her submission, but she wasn't his client, nor his responsibility. They were friends. Nothing more.

As for Vincent—he was her problem.

No one else's.

Jagger eyed the old wooden sign for *Olde Time Trinkets* as it danced in the air. A gust of wind blew by. It swung a little faster, creaking each time it swayed. This didn't seem like a good omen. Then again, this was New York in the heart of winter. Nothing would deter him from checking on Grace and pushing to get what he wanted most—her. Eventually, he'd wear her down. It was just a matter of time.

Tugging on the handle, he opened the door and entered the building. The bell dinged as the door slid shut behind him. A musty, slightly sour odor reached his nostrils. His nose wrinkled at the foul stench wafting in the air. He hadn't noticed it the last time he'd come by. What had they done in the last few days to cause this? Maybe something new and really old had arrived.

No. That couldn't be it. Something about the scent smelled familiar. The fumes were pungent, but he recognized them. How? He strode further into the room, inhaled a deep breath, and nearly choked on the putrefied fragrance. The shapeshifter he'd spotted a few blocks from here.

That's what this smelled like. Had the creature found its way into his female's shop?

Jagger stopped just near the register and scanned the shop. His gaze stopped on Grace, who worked on a display case to the right of the desk. Her eyes met his for a moment. Blatantly ignoring him, she turned back to the task at hand.

A low rumble resounded in his chest. He folded his arms across his chest. At the least, she deserved a lesson in politeness, but with the scent that lingered around them, he needed to finesse the situation. "Not even a greeting? What kind of customer service is that?"

"You're not a customer; just an annoying fly that won't go away."

He cocked an eyebrow. A smirk played at the corners of his mouth. Really? *A fly?* He was much more colorful than that. "A fly? I could see a rainbow stag beetle, but not a fly."

"Either way, you're still a pest," Grace snickered.

Oh, this bitch. She was really pissing him off. Jagger stalked across the store and closed the distance between them. He narrowed his dark green eyes at her. "You know, there are women who'd kill for my attention."

Grace rolled her eyes and flashed him a stiff smile. "Then go bug them. I have work—"

Hell, fuck no! Grabbing her arm, he jerked her against him. The doll in her hands fell to the floor with a slight thud. Even with her attitude, she was still the most beautiful woman he'd ever seen. Beautiful people deserved beautiful people. "You're the one I want. So, stop acting like we don't belong together."

"Let me go." Grace tugged her arm to get him to release his hold.

Except he refused. Not this time. He'd been as nice as he could be with her over the last year. No more. His grip on her arm tightened. "Agree to a date."

"Fuck you!" she spat at him. Despite the seething glare in her eyes, her gaze dropped to the floor.

This was the perfect opportunity for him to show her how much they belonged together. Jagger tucked a piece of loose hair behind her ear, gripped her chin, and forced her to look at him. Their eyes locked on one another. "You will give into me. Even if I have to make you."

Dipping his head, he closed his eyes and leaned in—her fist connected with his cheek. Although he didn't budge from his spot, a faint sting radiated through his jawline. His hold on her released.

The bell rang out as the front door opened and shut.

Her champagne-brown eyes hardened as she glowered at him. She shoved a finger in his face. "Come at me again and I'll make you squeal like a pig."

Jagger rubbed his jaw, making a show of her response. It didn't hurt, but it served him well to make her believe she'd caused him pain. This had now become a challenge. He loved those.

"Is there a problem?" Mr. Reddington asked from behind them.

Peering past Jagger, Grace blinked. She shifted her gaze back to him, narrowed her eyes, and crossed her arms. "No. He was just leaving."

Yes, he was. The corner of his mouth lifted. "This isn't over," he whispered. They were far from done. Not until he decided they were. Pivoting on the back of his heel, he nodded to Grace's father on his way out. He would get what he wanted. No matter what it took.

CHAPTER *five*

"THIS IS THE list of celebrities I've spoken to about judging. They're all on board." Vincent set down a sheet of paper on his boss's desk. Yesterday, his brunch with Grace proved how truly special and amazing she was. It made him want more: more of her time, her attention, of her. Period.

Which also meant he had to tell her the truth. He didn't want to start something with the lies between them. So, he'd come up with a plan. The first two phases had been easy to execute. All that remained was for his boss to choose a celebrity judge as his replacement.

While it left him to spend more time with Grace, it also ensured her manuscript got a fair shot. His last perusal confirmed all the names had gotten changed; no one could link anything back to his family. It was just like any other paranormal romance story.

"This is good," his boss, Henry, said. "There are several excellent options here."

"I agree. Let me know who you decide on. In the meantime, I'll touch base with legal, so we can cover any legal ramifications." Compensation may need to be considered, but primarily they'd want to assure the judge and author were properly protected.

"Give me a couple of hours. That'll give you enough time to get legal involved."

"Perfect. If you need nothing else from me, I've got a two-o'clock meeting to get to."

Henry waved him off, effectively dismissing him.

With a curt nod, Vincent stood and left his boss's office. He strode toward the elevators. As long as legal came through, everything would go off without a hitch. Those paper-pushers often took their sweet ass time with negotiations. Since they'd opted for a celebrity judge in the past, it should be quick and painless.

He hoped.

It didn't take long for the elevator doors to open. He rode the car three floors down, stepped off the elevator, and hooked a left toward his own office. Halfway there, his ears perked up at the nearby voices.

Vincent frowned. It couldn't be. His meeting with Chip was scheduled via telephone, but he absolutely heard the man nearby. Continuing on, he headed down the hallway that led to his office.

Just ahead, Aurora and Chip stood in front of his assistant's desk, happily chatting away. Neither seemed to notice his arrival. Or they didn't care.

Crossing his arms, he smirked. "Don't let me interrupt."

Chip turned in his direction and grinned. "Hey Vincent. I didn't see you come up."

Bullshit. He could read the lie on Chip's face. The words didn't quite reach his eyes. "I'm sure. Aren't we supposed to be meeting by phone?"

"That's probably my fault," Aurora said. "I needed to talk to him about something, so we met for lunch."

"Since I was already out this way, it made little sense to drive back to my office," Chip added.

He called *bullshit* again. The guy was up to something, but what? Vincent plastered a half-ass smile on his face and gestured to his office. "Well, then. Shall we?"

"Of course." Chip swung his gaze to Aurora. "It was good seeing you.

We'll talk again soon."

"Count on it."

Walking into his office, Vincent went straight to his desk. He heard a set of footsteps behind him, followed by the sound of the door closing.

"Stay the hell away from Grace."

Vincent stopped just to the side of his desk and spun on the heel of his shoe. "Excuse me?"

Chip folded his arms across his chest. "You damn well heard what I said."

Oh, yeah. He heard the words, all right. Not a single one of them made a bit of sense. How did Chip know he'd spent any time with Grace? How'd the guy even know Grace? Not once had she mentioned Chip—as a friend or other.

Narrowing his gaze, he scrutinized the young man. Chip's eyes sparkled with knowledge. Vincent frowned. He didn't like that—one bit. "What do you think you know?"

"I know a hell of a lot, including that you've shown up at her work multiple times, gone on two dates with her, and kissed her."

Vincent jerked his head back as he sat down. He would've sensed his own kin. All shapeshifters and kin were taught at an early age how to recognize it. "That's not possible."

"Why? Because you couldn't sense me? Did it ever occur to you that she told me about some of it? That I was in my car witnessing the kiss?" Chip leaned against the wall and crossed one ankle over the other.

His jaw clenched. All of that was highly probable. Not that it explained why Chip acted as if he had the right to choose who Grace dated. Vincent's upper lip curled. "Your point is?"

Pushing off the wall, Chip glared at him. "My point is she's kin, asshole. Stay. The. Hell. Away."

"Bullshit." The word left his mouth before he stopped it. Grace was special. He'd seen that for himself. Maybe he didn't fully understand it, but it didn't mean she was kin.

"Yeah, her father's human, but her mother was a shapeshifter. As Grace's ward, I'm telling you to leave her alone."

Her ward? With a snarl, Vincent exploded from the desk and jumped to his feet. "Are you fucking kidding me?"

Of all the things *not* to be mentioned, that was high on the priority list. Grace's ward should've approved all of their time together. He may be an outcast, but he still respected his people's ways. "Why the hell didn't she say anything?"

"Because she doesn't know, dipstick. Her mother died before teaching Grace about our world."

"Then why the hell didn't you?" Vincent spat out through gritted teeth. It didn't make a damn bit of sense. Grace was twenty-one. It was dangerous as hell for her not to be able to identify shapeshifters and hunters.

"*That* was what her mother wanted. I respected her wishes, just as I'm doing by ensuring Grace doesn't date a fucking shapeshifter. So, back off."

Vincent rubbed the back of his neck. His internal body temperature had risen a few degrees. The touch of his skin practically burned his hand, but it was a hell of a lot better than beating Chip, which was exactly what he wanted to do.

Not that it would change the situation. Grace was kin. Something he should've sensed, but hadn't. Why? Could his attraction to her have made an impact? Or maybe something else entirely had affected how he read her.

The reason mattered little. The male had ordered him to walk away. To leave behind the light in Grace's gentle, champagne eyes, her honeyed scent that smelled like home, her strong heart that beat in time to his own. Shaking his head, Vincent shifted his gaze to Chip. "I can't."

"Yes, you can. It's really simple. You walk away. Just. Like. This." Chip punctuated each of the last three words as he headed for the office door.

"No, I can't. She's my mate." He hadn't intended to share that bit of information; at least not yet, but he couldn't stop himself from admitting it. The last few days with Grace had shown him the truth, even if he still didn't believe he deserved her.

Chip froze. Turning around, he dragged a hand down his face. "Please tell me you're joking."

Vincent raised an eyebrow. Really? He'd never joke about something so serious. "Do I look like I'm joking?"

Lacing his fingers together, Chip snorted. "Fine. I believe you. Just know I expect you to keep me apprised of everything that goes on between you two." He held up a hand. "Minus intimate details. I don't really need to know that. Of course, that's if you can convince her to give you another chance."

"What're you talking about?" *Another chance?* How could she be upset when he hadn't seen her since yesterday? Come to think of it, she hadn't responded to any of his text messages or his phone call last night, either. Vincent growled. Shit. Chip's earlier words replayed in his mind. *"That I was in my car witnessing the kiss?"*

"Yeah. She already knows who you are, and that you lied to her."

"Son of a bitch!" Slamming his fist down on his desk, a loud roar escaped his mouth. Vincent's nostrils flared. He stepped from behind his desk and crossed his office in three long strides.

Most people cowered when his wolf showed itself. Not Chip. The guy didn't even take a step back. With a low snarl, Vincent got in Chip's face. "You need to fix this."

"No. *You're* the one who lied, so *you* need to fix it. If she's truly your mate, you'll figure it out." Chip sneered, opened the office door and walked out.

Grace dropped onto her couch and switched on the television. She didn't plan to watch anything, but it served as a great distraction. It had been almost twenty-four hours since she'd last spoken to Vincent. Minus the two-word text she'd sent an hour ago.

She sipped the Malbec in her wine glass and continued scanning through the channels. The man had a lot of nerve. Not once had he apologized for lying to her. Hell, he hadn't even admitted to his lies. His last message had read—

A knock at her door caught her attention. Setting her glass on the coffee table, she stood and ambled across her apartment. Whoever it was on the other side knocked louder. "Hold on. I'm coming."

For crying out loud. They had no patience. Grace opened the door. With a scowl, she raked her eyes over Vincent. Damn it. He shouldn't look that good in a three-piece dark blue suit when she was pissed at him. "What part of 'drop dead' did you misunderstand?"

He growled. "That's it? You're not even going to give me a chance to explain?"

"What's there to explain? You lied about who you are and what you do. Seems pretty clear to me. Or did I miss something?" *Arrogant ass.* If he hadn't lied about any of that, then there'd be something else in the future. That was just how liars worked.

Vincent gripped the back of his neck as his lips pinched together. "It's not that simple."

Her jaw slackened and her gaze fell to his unbuttoned white shirt. Why did he have to look so damn yummy? She was angry; no, that wasn't right. He'd hurt her. His lies caused her physical pain. There he stood, in all his gorgeousness, telling her it wasn't *that simple.* "Are you serious? It couldn't be any simpler if you tried. You're a fucking judge in a contest I entered. Something that important should've—"

Closing the distance between them, his large body filled the doorway and his lips crashed against hers.

Her body blossomed beneath his touch. Heat shot down her spine, igniting a fire in her belly. She grabbed his muscular biceps and pressed her body against his. *This is so wrong.* Not that she cared.

Wait. Yes, she did. No, she didn't. She really didn't. Not when he moved his mouth against hers like that and his tongue battled against her own. Nothing else mattered when their bodies were this entangled.

They moved further inside her apartment. The door slammed shut behind them. Vincent broke off the kiss and brushed a strand of her hair back. "I won't apologize for kissing you, but I needed you to stop talking and to listen to me. For just a second."

Damn it! He'd used their mutual attraction to gain entrance into her place. Grace jerked free of his arms. Her skin prickled with goosebumps. She backed up until there was at least six feet between them. It was the safest way to cool her body down. The betraying whore it was. "Say what you need to and get out."

He pinched the bridge of his nose, propped a hand on his hip and sighed. "I'm sorry I lied to you. When I came into your father's store last week, I came looking for you because of your manuscript. I didn't intend to lie, but I also didn't intend to be attracted to you, either."

My manuscript? Grace blinked. He'd read it? Did that have something to do with why he'd run off? No. That couldn't be it. Her eyes widened—the shock that had passed between them. He'd felt it. That current had left her thinking about him for the rest of that night. "Still doesn't explain why you lied."

"I was trying to protect myself. I've never had this kind of immediate chemistry with a woman before. I needed to figure it out before I could tell you the truth." Vincent dragged a hand through his soft blond locks. Hair she desperately wanted to run her fingers through.

Biting the inside of her bottom lip, her gaze met his. She could see the sorrow in his electric-blue eyes. Their normally bright hue had dulled. He looked like a child who'd lost a loved one. Grace inhaled and blew out the deep breath. She stared at the man across from her, drinking him in from head to toe. "Is that why you dragged me out of the restaurant Saturday night?"

"Yes. One of my coworkers came in and I wasn't prepared to answer questions."

She had noticed no one; then again, they'd left the restaurant so fast, there hadn't even been time to get their coats on. Physical attraction or not, she needed more than the genuine answers he'd provided thus far.

They'd talked about so much on their dates. How much of it had been a lie? All of it? Part of it? "Where did you get the name Leblanc?"

Closing his eyes, Vincent rubbed the middle of his forehead. With a slight grimace, he sighed. "It was my mother's maiden name."

Shaking her head, Grace paced back and forth in front of the television. With each step, her chest tightened a little more. She interlaced her fingers behind her back and clenched her jaw. "Why do I feel like having this conversation is like trying to get your last name all over again? You said you wanted to talk, but you don't appear all that thrilled to tell me the truth, either."

In the middle of her living room, she stopped and turned to face him. "You can't have it both ways. It's all, or it's nothing."

Vincent scrubbed his face. Exhaling a deep breath, he unbuttoned his suit jacket, walked over to the couch, and sat down. "I'm sorry. I'm not accustomed to talking about myself. I've spent years avoiding it."

What? He couldn't mean that literally. Grace blinked. Could he? Her mind drifted back to all the research she'd conducted on his publishing company. All editors of Nouveau Publishing House had social media accounts, except him. She'd located photographs and biographies for everyone, except him. He had truly hidden himself from the world.

Moving her wine glass out of the way, she sat on the coffee table across from him. "But I'm different."

"Yes."

"Why?" It made no sense. If he'd hidden from the world, then why didn't he hide from her as well? He'd lied about his identity, so why was he here now, trying to tell her the truth? What made her so special?

His electric-blue eyes met hers. He reached out tentatively, and then clasped her hand within his own. "You feel like home."

Home? Her breath caught in the back of her throat as her jaw slackened. Of all the things she expected him to say, that hadn't even registered. Her heart pounded inside her chest. Her belly fluttered as tingles shot down her spine.

He'd laid the bare truth out before her. What did she do with it? *Everything.* Both her body and heart jumped at the idea. Grace licked her lips. Except they still had a problem. One, neither of them could get around. She hung her head and stood. "You're still a judge. No matter what we're feeling… we just can't act on our emotions."

Vincent's lips curled into a smile. He got to his feet, grabbed her by the waist, and pulled her flush against his body. Dropping his voice low, he practically whispered, "What if I told you I'm not a judge anymore?"

What? Her eyes flicked to his. The electric-blue burned bright with hunger. Biting her bottom lip, she leaned into him. "Truly? But how?"

"Celebrity judge, and yes, my boss went for it." He caressed her cheek and brushed a soft kiss across her lips. "Think we can risk it now?"

CHAPTER *six*

"YES." A ONE-WORD answer escaped her mouth on a small gasp.

Closing his eyes, Vincent leaned his forehead against hers and breathed in deeply.

His breath on her face tickled ever so slightly. Not that she minded. He smelled like a sweet mix of woods and masculine tang. Grace swallowed. Recalling their last kiss, he tasted like nothing that had ever hit her palate and she was ready for more.

"I hope this means you forgive me." His lips curled into a broad grin as he stroked her cheek with his knuckles.

Grace canted her head. How could she not? His demeanor with every question she'd asked had proven his honesty. "You've been sincere with your answers. I can see it in your face. Just… no more lies. Please?"

Talk about a crack in the veneer. There she stood, asking *him* not to lie to her when she had a secret of her very own.

Vincent's brow furrowed. "I promise to tell you everything I can."

Grace's shoulders tensed. That wasn't the answer she'd hoped for. Was she being hypocritical, asking him for no more lies when she hadn't uttered one word about her visions? Her lips pressed together. With a tiny grimace, she moved to step out of his arms. She was an idiot for thinking this could work. That *this* relationship could be different.

He tightened his grip around her waist. Vincent sighed. "I won't always be able to tell you things, like with my job. Sometimes it requires discretion while negotiations are going on, but I promise I'll spend every moment we have together showing you I'm a good man."

Her gaze leveled on him. What was wrong with her? Yeah, he hadn't been entirely honest with his identity, but she wasn't being honest either. "I believe you. In fact—"

"That makes me happy." Cupping her face, he brushed a soft kiss across her lips. "*Thrilled*."

"Oh?" Shivers ran down the back of her spine. A sensation that never got old, but she couldn't let it distract her. She had to tell him. Grace skated a hand up his arm and stroked the nape of his neck.

Vincent growled. His head slanted as his mouth covered hers. He swept his tongue along the seam of her lips and plied her mouth open.

As the kiss deepened, he ran one hand up and down her back, spearing his fingers through her caramel-colored locks. His firm body pressed closer to hers.

Every hard edge of his felt so good. Her fingers curled around the back of his neck as she pulled him flush against her curves. She moaned into the kiss. His touch sent shock after shock to her synapses, lighting her entire body ablaze.

Releasing the kiss, both of them panted. Vincent's gaze dropped to hers, his blue eyes dark with desire. He looked at her as if she were his next meal.

Grace swallowed, her admission all but forgotten, as a jolt of electricity shot straight to her core. Her hand grazed his collarbone near the open collar of his button-down shirt. She threaded her fingers into his short dirty-blond hair and tugged his mouth back to hers. She stroked the inside of his mouth with her tongue.

A beast of an erection pressed into her belly. She moaned at the idea of him buried inside of her. The thought of them joined together set her on fire. All she could think about was having him—all of him.

Vincent's fingertips skated along the small of her back, playing with the hem of her t-shirt. He trailed soft kisses across her jawline and down her throat.

The feathery touch sent tingles all over her body. His hands made her feel beautiful, even in jeans and a t-shirt. She couldn't stand the thought of not having him naked and in her bed any longer.

"God, I want you," Grace whispered huskily.

Lifting his eyes to hers, he nuzzled her nose. "Are you sure?"

"Yes." Just to prove how much, she leaned back, grabbed the bottom of her t-shirt, and swept it over her head. In one move, she revealed the simple black bra covering the soft curve of her ample breasts. If she could wriggle free, she'd take off her pants too. By the look on his face, it wasn't necessary. Yet.

His eyes widened and he swallowed as he drank in the sight of her. "You're stunning."

"And you're overdressed." Grace bit her bottom lip. She wanted him more than she'd ever wanted anyone. Reaching up to the lapels of his jacket, she pushed it free from his broad shoulders.

Nothing could stop this from happening. There was no need to rush, but she wanted to see more of him. Every inch of him. She fumbled slightly with the buttons on his shirt, but continued to work through them.

Vincent pulled the shirt from his pants, shrugged it off his shoulders, and let it fall to the couch behind them.

Seeing his golden skin in all its glory, from his chiseled pecs to his well-defined eight-pack, sent a flash of heat coursing through her body. Grace gently dragged her hands up his ripped abs, over his powerful chest and shoulders, and down his taut arms. She followed the same path again with tender kisses until she reached his neck. The sweet tang of orange hit her palate.

His lips locked on hers. Vincent crushed his body against hers. His lips left hers and skimmed across her jaw, down her throat, and on her collarbone. He tugged one bra-strap off her right shoulder and yanked the covering away from her breast. With a small growl, Vincent's mouth latched onto her nipple.

Grace moaned, her head falling back. Heat blazed over her as he devoured her like she was the oxygen to his lungs. A current of electricity shot straight to her core, dampening her panties.

Tugging a strap from her left shoulder, he sucked on her other nipple and unhooked her bra. It slid to the floor.

The electric-blue of his eyes darkened with an uncontrollable need. He growled, grabbed her by the ass, and hefted her off the floor.

Her denim-clad legs wrapped around his waist as he ground the length of his hardness right at her core. Fisting a handful of her hair, Vincent nipped at her lips, deepening the kiss as he carried her directly to the bedroom.

Once he got close enough, he dropped her on her bed. His mouth latched onto a nipple again. Her back arched, moaning at the way his tongue teased her. The lashing vibrated through her body. It wiped away all thought. There was nothing but him on her mind.

The tips of Vincent's fingertips skated along the side of her breast and her delicate waistline. He unbuttoned her jeans and licked a line to the top of her waistband. Unzipping her pants, he drew them over her hips and peeled them slowly down her legs.

His lips trailed a path along one bare leg and then back up the other. Vincent's hooded gaze fell to hers. "You're so beautiful."

Grace swallowed. His kind words didn't unnerve her, but the way he looked at her spoke volumes. Almost as if he planned to eat her alive. Her belly fluttered as another blast shot to her core. "Fuck, Vincent."

In one swift move, he yanked her simple black panties from her body and growled at the sight of her. Sliding his hands up the back of her legs, he buried his face right at the apex of her thighs.

"Oh, God!" Her fingers tangled in his hair, tugging at him as he licked at her already swollen clit. His tongue was like magic, while his hands danced across her body as if it were his own personal playground.

He sucked and licked her, bringing her to the edge, then slowed his pace and did it all over again. Vincent pressed a kiss to her thigh and dove his tongue back into her. One hand came up and kneaded her breast.

"Vincent," Grace whimpered. She was so close. Her body pulsed. He pinched her nipple and sent her flying. Her body shook and convulsed as the orgasm that had been just out of reach barreled through her.

Holy shit. Vincent lapped at her until he swallowed every drop she had to give. Lifting his head, his eyes met hers as he wiped around his mouth. He sucked on his fingers.

Even half-dressed, staring at her the way he did, despite the orgasm he'd just given her, her body heated, primed for him. With a groan, she bit her bottom lip and arched her back.

He growled. Coming to his full height, Vincent kicked off his shoes, undid his buckle and pants, and then shucked his remaining clothes to the floor.

Standing there completely naked, Grace gasped as her gaze landed on his cock and shifted back to his face. Holy fuck! Would he even fit inside her? She wasn't petite, but she wasn't big either. Oh, but she couldn't wait to find out. She licked her lips, crooked a finger at him, and gave him her best come-hither look. "Yum."

His arousal hardened more, aimed right at her. A mischievous smile crossed his face as he crawled up her body. He pressed a kiss to her thigh, her belly, and nuzzled her breast before he reached her mouth. "You don't say."

"Yes, I do." Her lips fused to his, and she pushed her tongue inside his mouth. She didn't know where the desire had come from, but she just had to know what they tasted like together.

He groaned into the kiss. Vincent gripped her hips and drove his cock into her slit until they were fully connected to the hilt. He shuddered. "Fuck."

"Oh, God, Vincent," Grace cried out. It was a good thing she hadn't thought too much about his girth. They hadn't even moved and her toes had already curled. It was only bound to get better. Her legs hooked together behind his ass, and she gyrated her hips.

With a loud growl, he tightened his hold on her hips and pistoned in and out of her. "Fuck, you feel good."

"Don't stop." Grace grabbed him by the biceps and dug in her nails. She could feel him all over, as if every stroke of his cock marked her. Their mixed moans and the slick sheen of sweat between them had her burning from the inside out.

He pounded into her hard and deep, holding nothing back. Her body rocked under his. Lowering his head, he latched onto one of her breasts and nipped at her nipple.

"Vincent!" Her nails scratched down his back as her inner walls clenched around his rigid length. A powerful orgasm rolled through her and sent him right over the edge into his own.

He drilled into her until she milked the last drop of his orgasm and nothing but their ragged breathing filled the air. Vincent brushed a soft kiss across her lips and swept the hair from her face.

Grace beamed up at him. "That was amazing."

"You say the sweetest things." He grinned. His electric-blue eyes brightened, telling her he'd never let her go.

Not that she wanted him to.

"What are you thinking about?" Vincent asked as he lazily stroked Grace's naked back. Her head rested comfortably against his chest. They finished a second round about a half hour ago and relaxed into one another's arms. He'd never been much into snuggling, but with her… he didn't want to be anywhere else.

She placed her chin on his pectoral muscle and looked at him. "You said I feel like home. Did you mean to say that?"

No lies. That's what he told himself. He hadn't meant to admit it, but now that it was out there, he wouldn't take it back. Not a single word. That wasn't what she asked him, though. "No."

"Did you mean it?"

"I did." It had just been a long time since he had a home. He had a place to rest his head. A place to be away from work. A place to clean up, but it hadn't been home in years.

Grace's brows furrowed. "I don't understand."

He had lived in this city his whole life. For the longest time, he had everything—friends, family, a sense of belonging. That all changed not long after his nineteenth birthday until he met her. How did he explain that? Without scaring her off. Still skimming his fingers up and down her back, Vincent stared at the ceiling. "I've been alone since my parents died. Almost eleven years ago."

She pressed a loving kiss to his chest, right where his heart beat beneath his ribs. All of her emotions conveyed in a single touch. "I'm sorry that you did. I can't imagine the pain you must've felt."

It had been agony. He'd shut down for a bit after they were gone. Time and anger had finally motivated him. The driver that caused the accident had survived and disappeared. His parents might've lived through the accident if their car hadn't caught on fire. Shapeshifters heal fast, but even they couldn't heal from that kind of damage. Vincent flicked his eyes back to the ceiling. "I don't think we ever truly recover from that kind of loss. We just go through the motions until we're pulled in a new direction."

"Is that what you see with me? A new direction?"

"I do, but I think it's more than that." He didn't know how to explain it. His earlier statement had been the simplest explanation, but in his heart, it went deeper. She'd torn down walls he'd put in place. Filled holes he'd forgotten existed. Gave life to a heart he believed to be dead and cold. Breathed oxygen into his empty lungs. In just a few short days, she'd reminded him what it was like to live.

His gaze dropped to hers. Her champagne orbs shined like the stars. Vincent swallowed. He could drown in the warmth of her eyes. When she looked at him like that, it was like being enveloped in the sun. He caressed her cheek. "When I look at you, it's like I never lost them."

"If you tell me, I remind you of your mother, I will hurt you." Grace smirked.

Vincent bust out in laughter. She didn't remind him of his mother. Not in any way. They looked nothing alike. His mother had been blonde and tall for a woman. Not to mention she'd been a shapeshifter. But she had also been demure. His laughter faded as he dropped his gaze to Grace's face. She was fire. Passionate and sarcastic in the best way possible.

Wrapping his arm around her waist, he rolled her over to her back and brushed a kiss first against her lips, and then her neck and collarbone. "You're definitely nothing like my mother."

"That's good because otherwise… this would've gotten creepy real fast." Her words dripped with sarcasm.

He cracked a grin and nuzzled the dip between her breasts. "You tease me in the worst way, woman."

"Who's teasing who?" She arched her back and dragged her nails down his back.

He growled. His cock hardened at the little prickles of pain she created with her fingers. Vincent slipped his fingers inside of her sex. With his thumb, he rubbed her clit and fused his lips to hers. He'd never grow tired of her sweet and succulent taste.

Grace moaned into the kiss as their tongues entangled and hooked a leg around the back of his ass. She ground against his fingers.

Once he had her primed, he removed his fingers, sucked her glistening wetness from them and drove his cock deep inside of her, taking her again.

Last night had been an experience. One he wouldn't forget anytime soon. Although he had her three times last night, he'd taken her again this morning in the shower. He just couldn't get enough. Vincent stared at

Grace in her light pink bra and matching panties. She looked gorgeous standing there as she yanked a pair of jeans from her closet.

"I think you should stay just like this." Coming up behind her, he pressed a soft kiss behind her ear and wrapped his arms around her body.

With a brief chuckle, she brushed her lips against the warmth of his arm. "Really? You want me to go to class and work half-naked?"

That wasn't what he had in mind. Vincent growled and hugged her tightly against him. "No."

She busted out in laughter and spun to face him. Reaching up, Grace stroked the back of his neck. "I didn't think so. Now, can I finish getting dressed?"

"If you must." He sighed. Honestly, he wouldn't mind another round with her, but they both had places to be and things to take care of.

"Yes, I must." Smirking, she turned back to her closet to peruse through her clothing options.

Seeing her like that in her all her honey-tasting deliciousness made him want to take a bite. He wasn't certain she'd appreciate that, though. So, he went for the next best option and smacked her ass.

Grace yelped and peered over her shoulder at him.

Vincent lounged against the edge of her bed, grinning like a Cheshire cat. "What? I did nothing."

"Right." Grace rolled her eyes, pointed her forefinger at him and tugged her jeans over her legs. Shaking her head, she grabbed one of her *Book Nerd* t-shirts and pulled it over her head. She left the bedroom and headed for the kitchen.

Such a shame to cover all her tastiness up. He had on the same dark blue pants from the day before, along with his white button-up shirt. He'd have to make a trip home for a quick shower and change of clothes before heading into the office. It was all worth it for what they'd shared last night.

Vincent followed Grace and opened her microwave. He handed her a plate with a breakfast burrito.

"Where'd that come from?"

"I threw it together while you were drying your hair." It had taken little effort. He'd just been grateful she had the most important ingredients: tortilla shell, eggs, sausage, and cheese.

She tilted her head and cracked a smile. "I feel like after last night, I should make *you* breakfast."

"Ah, yes, but you don't have time for that this morning. I promise, if it'll make you feel better, you can make me breakfast next time." Vincent took her hand in his and escorted her to her living room. He'd laid out a glass of orange juice, water, a napkin, a fork, and a knife on the wooden coffee table. A dining room table would've been preferable, but she didn't have one in her loft-style apartment. Really, it was something that needed to be rectified.

"You did all this?"

"Yes." His gaze flicked from her to the spread on the table and back again. Her reaction shouldn't have surprised him, but it did. He had given little thought to her previous relationships. It had been a long time since he'd been in one, but he couldn't imagine sending her off to class without a full belly. Vincent sat on the couch next to her.

A smile tugged at the corners of her lips. "Thank you. This is really considerate of you."

"I wouldn't have it any other way." He leaned forward, his elbows digging into his thighs as he watched her take the first bite.

"Mm, this is fantastic." Grace chewed and swallowed the food in her mouth. "Are you going to watch me eat the whole time?"

It had been his plan. Based on that question, maybe he should reconsider it. Vincent raised an eyebrow. "Is there something wrong with me watching you eat?"

"Well, one, it makes me feel guilty when you're not eating. And, two, it makes me a little self-conscious. What if I drool? Or I drop something on my t-shirt?" She leveled a stare at him.

He chuckled. She was so damn adorable. Standing, Vincent shook his head. "I prepared one for myself, but I was going to let you eat first. I'll get mine if it makes you feel better."

Her cheeks flushed. "Yes, it would."

With a quick nod, he stepped around the coffee table and started toward the kitchen. A picture hanging on the wall to the right of the television caught his attention. He stopped in front of the photograph and narrowed his eyes. *It couldn't be.* A younger Grace sat on a picnic blanket with an older woman—a woman he recognized.

Vincent glanced over his shoulder at Grace and back to the picture. How had he missed it? Same brown hair. Same bright, champagne-colored eyes. Same high cheekbones. He swallowed and recalled what Chip had said the day before. *"Yeah, her father's human, but her mother was a shapeshifter."*

Closing his eyes, he dragged a hand through his hair. He had to ask. He had to be sure. "Hey, uh, Grace. Who's this woman in the photo with you?"

"That's my mom. She died…"

Eleven years ago, he finished in his head. He didn't need to hear the rest of what she said to know the answer. He'd been there. Or at least he'd seen the aftermath. The memory of that night flooded his brain.

His paws pounded against the forest floor as he led the members of his pack to the clearing. It had taken longer than it should've to locate the pack. They just had to get to the—Vincent's eyes narrowed as he spotted the clearing ahead. The metallic scent hit his nostrils. His speed increased, the echo of his pack following suit resounded loudly in his ears.

Six sets of feet stampeding through the forest with one person in mind—their alpha. Although they could communicate, none of them did. They all simply wanted to reach her.

Despite being the youngest, he was also the largest and fastest, which meant he reached her first. The beta, Phil, was just behind him, followed by the rest of his pack—Derek, Amir, Ethan, and Lucian.

Vincent skidded to a stop and crouched down. He nudged Maddie with his nose, but the naked female didn't move. No, she couldn't be gone. With a firmer nudge, he tried once again to stir her, but she didn't rise.

"Is she…" he heard in his mind. Phil's gray-blue fur appeared in his line of

sight. "Vincent? She's gone, isn't she?"

The blood seeping from the gaping wound in her gut should've been his first indicator. The unusual angle of her neck—that should've been his second. Vincent hung his head. He'd left her... to die.

"We can't leave her like this," Derek's voice echoed in his mind.

"Let's get her out of here and you can tell us what happened when we get back to camp," Phillip said.

It had been a sight no shapeshifter should be forced to see. His pack had exiled him after that, believing he'd been at fault for Maddie's death. He had been the one to leave her alone with a hunter. Vincent glanced back over his shoulder to find Grace standing in front of him.

She stared at him wide-eyed. "Are you okay? You zoned out for a couple of minutes there."

"Yeah, sorry. I guess I just got lost in my own thoughts." He gestured to the picture. "Your mother, she... she just looks like someone I used to know."

"Oh?" Grace canted her head at him. "She did work at the Epiphany Library for several years. It's possible you may have crossed paths with her."

"I suppose so." It was as close to the truth as he could get without explaining his wolf and exactly how he knew Grace's mother. Vincent plastered a smile on his face and peered at the half-eaten burrito on the coffee table. He draped an arm around Grace's shoulders, hugged her to his body, and pressed a kiss to her forehead. "Go finish eating while I get mine."

Pulling back from the hug, she lifted her champagne orbs to him again. "Are you sure you're okay?"

"Yeah, I'm good. I promise." Vincent cupped her chin and brushed his lips across hers. He watched for a moment as she returned to her spot on the couch. With no further objections, he strode across the way to the kitchen.

There would come a time when he'd have to tell her the truth. Until then, he'd savor every second they had together, because she may not forgive him once she knew what happened.

CHAPTER *seven*

GRACE GRUNTED UNDER the weight of the box in her arms. What idiot packed a box this size full of lamps? The bell at the front of the store rang. Of course someone would choose this moment to shop.

"I'll be with you in a second," she called out. Provided she could get this box where it belonged. Grace readjusted her load and started for the cart. Damn it, why didn't she bring it closer?

"Why is it whenever I come in you're always making me wait?" Vincent asked as he easily took the box from her hands. "Where do you want this?"

Wiping the sweat from her brow, she gestured to the cart five feet away. "I made you wait one time."

"Two, actually. You weren't even here the second time I came in." He smirked and set the box down on the cart as if it weighed nothing.

"You can't blame me for that. You just have the worst timing ever." Grace cracked a grin as she grabbed the handles and pushed the cart out of the storage room. Maybe his timing before had been off, but today it had been impeccable. It would've taken her at least another three minutes to get the box onto the cart, if not longer.

Vincent followed her. "I always thought I had perfect timing."

"Keep telling yourself that and it might just come true." She hadn't had this much fun bantering with someone in a long time. Even before that first date, getting Vincent all riled up had been enjoyable. He gave it to her as much as she dished it out.

Their relationship was almost perfect. Except they each had secrets. She was sure of it. Vincent had spent too much time focused on the picture of her and her mother this morning. Not that she had any clue why.

But she wouldn't begrudge him for not saying anything, even if she had made him promise no more lies. She hadn't exactly told him her secret, either. She just had to find the right moment.

"I think it already has."

Grace shook her head, extracted a box cutter from the back pocket of her jeans, and opened the box. "Not that I'm not happy to see you, but to what do I owe this pleasure?"

Coming up behind her, he removed the box cutter from her hand, set it aside, and spun her around to face him. Vincent caressed her cheek. "Why do I need a reason to see you?"

Shivers ran down her spine as she tilted her head back. Gripping the cart behind her, Grace swallowed. "It doesn't mean you don't have one."

"Maybe I just wanted to steal a kiss." He wrapped his arms around her waist and crushed her to his body. Leaning his head down, Vincent's lips fused with hers. His tongue stroked the inside of her mouth.

She moaned into the kiss. Pressing in tighter, she slid her hands up his back and dug her nails into his shoulder blades. Heat blazed through her veins as their tongues battled. Grace had been so ingrained in the moment; she hadn't heard the bell ring as the store's front door opened.

The chime of the bell tickled his ears, but it wasn't what caught his attention. The smell of damp moss permeated his nose. Vincent released the kiss and flicked his eyes toward the scent. His gaze landed on a lithe man with jet black hair and unsettling forest-green eyes.

A man he recognized.

He'd never forgotten the hunter's scent or looks. It may have been years, but his life changed forever that day. Vincent shuffled Grace behind him. It was her world, but she knew nothing about it. It may not stop a fight, but he wouldn't take that chance. His eyes glowed, his fangs elongated, and he growled at the hunter.

"What are you doing?" Grace asked as she attempted to muscle her way from behind him.

The hunter's cold, green eyes narrowed as he reached behind him, possibly for a weapon. He adjusted his stance and snarled at Vincent. "You won't get away this time."

Did the guy have a concealed weapon? It was highly likely. He couldn't completely shift, not in front of Grace. There were supposed to be rules, but he suspected those wouldn't be followed. Not today.

He had to do what was necessary to protect her. With one hand behind him, Vincent grabbed her hip and sidestepped until the nearby aisle was at their backs. He peered at her from the corner of his eye. "Go to the storage room and lock the door."

"But—"

"Just do it!" He didn't have time to argue with her over this. His ears perked at the sound of her sneakers squeaking across the wooden floor. He glanced over his shoulder in time to see the back-door slam shut. One less thing—

Taking the hunter's shoulder to the gut, Vincent grimaced. The guy had lunged at him and he'd been distracted just enough to miss the move. But he wasn't the same kid he'd been back then. He drove his knee into the hunter's chest and sent him flying into the front counter.

Landing by the edge of the counter, the hunter jumped to his feet and charged at Vincent again.

He readjusted his stance and prepared for another shoulder check. What he got instead was an uppercut to the jaw that knocked him to the floor.

"Jagger! Stop it!" Grace screamed.

A low growl rumbled from the hunter's throat as his eyes flicked from Grace to Vincent. "This isn't over, mutt."

Damn it! Vincent looked up. Why the hell had she come out? He pointed to the storage room. "Get back in there."

The sound of heavy steps echoed across the wooden floor as Vincent got to his feet. He stood in time to see the front door swing shut. He took off down the center aisle, stormed out of the store, and glanced each way along the sidewalk.

Nothing.

Leaning his head back slightly, he sniffed the air. The grime of the city clogged his nostrils. Instead of the damp moss scent he'd sought, he only smelled the stench of sweat, overbearing sweet perfumes, the spice of dark roasted coffee, and exhaust fumes.

Vincent coughed a few times to clear the conglomeration of smells from his nose. *Shit. Shit. Shit.* He'd lost the hunter. Rewinding the last few minutes in his head, he frowned. Wait a second. Grace had given the hunter a name. Did she know him?

Shaking the final scents away, he scrubbed his face. His eyebrows were still a little bushy. A quick check of his teeth and nose confirmed the rest of his face had returned to normal.

He headed back inside and found Grace exactly where he'd left her—standing in the middle of the aisle with all the lamps. "Are you okay?"

Her hands fidgeted as she glanced from him to the front door and back again. "What the hell just happened?"

How did he explain this to her? Though he had to tell her about their world soon, he never expected it to be *this* soon. Vincent opened his mouth and snapped it shut. Shit. He didn't even know where to begin.

Grace held up a hand and shook her head. "If you won't tell me the truth, then don't even waste your breath. I saw your face, for fuck's sake. It sure as hell didn't look like what it does now. And Jagger… I've never seen him like that!"

With a heavy sigh, Vincent pinched the bridge of his nose. "Calm down. I'll tell you everything… just not here."

"It's not like there's anyone around." She gestured to the empty store.

"That doesn't mean it'll remain that way, and this isn't something that can be told in a few minutes." Not to mention, she'd likely freak out the second he revealed his wolf. She'd caught a glimpse, a small fraction of what he would look like in his full form, and that had caused some obvious tension in her shoulders.

"Then what do you suggest?"

He dragged a hand through his hair. That was a good question. They needed privacy for this conversation. Definitely not neutral ground. The work crew had completed the last changes to his house yesterday. Maybe… it had been his original plan, after all. "Why don't you come over for dinner tonight? I can explain it all then."

She crossed her arms and blew a loose strand of hair from her face. "Fine, but I expect a complete explanation."

"Understood." With that he walked over to the front counter, sat in the chair he'd seen Grace's father occupy, and removed his cell phone from his pocket.

"Um, what do you think you're doing?" She strode down the aisle and stopped in front of the counter.

"I'm making myself comfortable." Vincent grinned. No way in hell was he leaving her alone with a hunter on the loose. He'd get all the information necessary about *Jagger* over dinner, and then he'd do something he hadn't done in years—patrol.

"But I'm at work."

"I know." That wouldn't deter him. Not for one second.

With an exasperated groan, Grace threw her hands in the air. "Fine. Just stay out of the way."

Jagger eyed the grotesque worm as it exited *Olde Time Trinket.* He pressed his body closer to the brick wall, blending into the alley's shadows. He hadn't expected to find that *thing* in the store, nor had he anticipated seeing it kissing his woman. While he could've taken the creature, he'd gone into the shop unprepared. Something that wouldn't happen again. Especially not where Grace was concerned.

She knew nothing about his world. It was far too soon to bring her into it. Though she absolutely required protection from it. He glowered as the shapeshifter sniffed the air and returned to the shop. "Damn it," he muttered.

The creature should've left, chased after him even. He'd planned to go back to the shop once it had gone by and disappeared from his sight. How the hell had this thing even gotten involved with Grace? That didn't matter. He had to get it away from her. Then once he had her alone, learn everything he could and properly dispose of it this time.

Jagger dug his cell phone out of the back pocket of his jeans. He called up the contact list and depressed Laurent's number. The phone rang. He grounded his teeth as it rang a second and third time. Where the fuck was he?

On the fourth ring, Laurent answered, "Hello?"

"Go to my place, get my gear, and get your ass here to Grace's shop," he snapped. "Now!"

"Alright, alright. I'm on it," his friend squeaked.

Growling, Jagger disconnected the line and shoved his phone into the back pocket of his jeans. Tonight, they took care of business. That freak wouldn't escape him a second time.

"That's really all you know about him?"

"For the fiftieth time, yes. His name is Jagger Vautour and he's purchased one item from the store in the past year." They had spent the last hour discussing that douchebag. Although something *had* gone on between Vincent and Jagger, they hadn't even broached that subject.

"You have any idea what brought him into the store today?"

Grace rolled her eyes as Vincent pulled the Lincoln into an extended driveway. She shifted her gaze to the house. Something about the one-story Victorian-style house seemed vaguely familiar. "Probably the same reason he always comes in."

"Which is?"

"To ask me out, despite the number of times I've turned him down. He doesn't seem to understand the term *no.* Sound like someone you know?" She flicked her eyes to Vincent and narrowed her gaze. He'd sort of asked her out twice without taking no for an answer.

"Not at all." Flashing his teeth, he parked the car and shut off the ignition.

"Right." Her one-word answer dripped with sarcasm as she climbed out of the vehicle. Grace walked around the front of the car and headed directly for the side entrance she somehow knew existed.

"I mean, I got the date. He didn't." Vincent strolled beside her and unlocked the door to let her in.

"That's because you didn't give me a choice." She stepped over the threshold and stopped halfway to the living room. What the hell? Why did she have this sense of déjà vu? As if she had been to Vincent's house before.

The chef-styled kitchen sat to her right, complete with a granite-top island. Three bedrooms in total were down the hall, two on the left side of the house, and the master on the right, next to the second bathroom. Grace headed further into the living room. No Christmas decorations anywhere. She reached out and ran her hand along the soft material of the deep blue couch. *This is new.*

She glanced over her shoulder at the dining room, situated to the right of the back door. A brand-new mahogany table seating four had taken the place of the antique dining-room table made for a large family. *How do I know all of this?*

"You okay?" Vincent asked from the kitchen as he removed the various contents of their dinner order from the brown paper bag.

Grace shook her head. "I feel like I'm replaying something in my mind, but I can't quite get a grasp on it."

"Like a memory?"

"Yeah." But it didn't explain how she remembered this place. She'd never been to his house before. Maybe she'd seen it a few years back when she'd been looking for her own place. No, that made little sense. Vincent had told her he'd lived here all of his life.

There had to be some plausible explanation. Maybe she had seen a layout like this one. That could be it. Grace wandered around the living room. No pictures hung on the walls, and none sat on the mantel below the mounted television. Weird, she remembered a house like that. She continued walking around and stopped in front of a spot on the wall where height lines had been marked.

Grace reached out and touched the six-foot-three scribbled on the corner of the wall. The second her fingers hit the vanilla-colored surface, her mind's eye opened.

"Just breathe through it, son," a male voice said in her head.

"The first shift is always the hardest," a female voice added.

Vincent laid on the forest ground, naked, with a sheen of sweat covering his body. He cried out as a sickening pop echoed all around them. His arms and legs shortened in length. His nose and mouth stretched as his canines elongated. He howled in pain. The dimensions of his body altered with several more snaps and pops. His dirty-blond hair spanned his entire body and grew to white fur.

After a moment, the moaning ceased. Vincent shakily stood on four paws. He was no longer a man, but a massive wolf. His electric-blue gaze turned as if he was looking right at her.

She gasped and yanked her hand from the wall.

"What have you… oh, I see you found my growth chart," Vincent said. He shuffled from her side to the dining room with their food in hand.

What the hell did I just see? Grace peered over her shoulder and watched Vincent set up the Chinese food cartons as if nothing had happened.

Granted, he didn't know she had visions, but that didn't ease her mind at all.

If what she'd just seen was true, then he was a beast. An honest-to-God beast.

Not something she thought she'd ever cross in her lifetime. Grace swallowed. What had she gotten herself into? She was locked in a house she somehow recognized with a beast because he insisted on driving them back to his place. And she had allowed it to happen. She'd seen the slight change in his face earlier and she'd still gotten into the car.

What is wrong with me? She had every intention of making him explain what had gone down that afternoon. Instead, he'd distracted her with question after question about Jagger.

Wait… Jagger had attacked Vincent first. Grace blinked.

"Are you planning to stand over there all night? Or were you going to join me for dinner?" Vincent asked.

That was a damn good question. She just didn't know how to answer it.

Grace didn't move. Nor did she answer his question.

He thought he'd heard an audible gasp when her fingers had grazed the wall a few minutes ago, but he couldn't confirm it. The hunter had all of his focus as he figured out a plan of attack. Vincent got to his feet and crossed the living room to where Grace remained planted. "Are you okay?"

"I honestly don't know how to answer that."

What? How could she not know? Had she realized she knew the house? Vincent gripped the back of his neck. He'd hoped with the change of décor that it wouldn't look familiar. "Are you saying you don't know how you feel?"

"No. I'm saying I have so many emotions running through me right now that I can't decide which one to focus on first."

Oh. He didn't like the sound of that. How could she have—who was he kidding? He already knew the answer to that. She had figured out something was off with him. She likely recognized the house, despite the changes to the furniture. Of course she would. She'd written a fucking manuscript about his parents.

There was only one thing he could do. Vincent reached out to wrap her in arms, but she stepped back from him. He frowned. He should've seen this coming, but it didn't stop the ache any less.

Grace shook her head. "No. You do *not* get to distract me from the mess in my head."

"I wasn't trying to distract you. I thought if I comforted you, then maybe you could… decipher what you're feeling." He had missed something. A sign or a moment where she'd seen something, an item, a piece of furniture, or something to make her confused.

Grinding her teeth, Grace crossed her arms and scoffed. "You thought a hug would help me sort my feelings? Right. Sure, that's exactly what it would do. It'd help me rightfully express my anger or the ache in my heart or the panic running through my mind as I conclude that I'm an idiot."

Vincent blinked. Her words caught him completely off guard. That wasn't what he thought she'd say at all. With all those different emotions, he believed she was about to point out the obvious. He dragged a hand through his hair. "I don't follow."

"Right, so you want me to explain? Okay, I'll explain." Each word she spat out tenser than the last. Grace stomped around him and placed her hand on the couch.

"From the moment we pulled onto your street, everything looked familiar. For the life of me, I couldn't figure out why. In fact, for a second, I questioned my sanity. I knew every detail of this house. Then it finally hit me. I described it all in my manuscript. Just not the furniture because you read my manuscript and changed everything. Oh, I know you got another judge, so it would have a fair shot, but why bother if you would not admit to reading my story? I suspect if you hadn't, you wouldn't have come looking for me. Right?"

Grimacing, Vincent dropped his gaze to his feet. Damn it. He should've admitted this to her last night or even told her about it this morning. He'd gotten so caught up with everything and that was one of those things he hadn't gotten around to telling her. Vincent sighed. "Yes, I read your manuscript. Yes, I replaced the furniture."

"And didn't bother to tell me. I'd ask why, but I'm pretty sure it has something to do with my manuscript itself. I mean, you couldn't admit to reading it, right? Because then I would've asked why you came looking for me. Then you'd have to explain you're not entirely human. That you're a monster, a beast, and Jagger saw that in you, and he was just—"

"Don't you dare think for one fucking second that he was trying to protect you!" Vincent growled. He would deal with being called *a monster*, even *a beast*, but under no circumstances would he accept the asinine idea a hunter was out to keep her safe. "He'd have killed you the second he realized who you were. Jagger is a hunter, and he hunts shapeshifters, my kind, and their kin."

"Shapeshifters? That makes no sense. Why would he come after me? I'm not either. I'm only in this world because of you, a world you decided not to tell me anything about." Grace leveled her champagne eyes at him.

"Bullshit! I had nothing to do with any of that. It was all your mother's doing." The words had left his mouth before he could stop them. He didn't plan to throw Maddie under the bus, but it just kind of happened. Not that he could take it back now.

"Excuse me! My mother wasn't—"

"Oh, yes, she fucking was. She was my alpha." Fucking hell, someone stick a fork in his tongue. Admission after admission kept coming out of his mouth. There were some things Grace absolutely could not know.

"No, no. You're talking crazy. I don't believe any of this. Shapeshifters. Kin. Hunters… none of it." Rubbing at her brow, Grace waved off his statements as her shoulders slumped.

"It is true and I'll prove it." He had no choice. He had to make her see the truth. Vincent unbuttoned his shirt, untucked it from his pants, and stripped.

"What are you doing?"

"I prefer not to ruin a good suit." He tossed his clothes aside and with a low snarl, he released his wolf. His bones snapped and popped as they rearranged in length and mass. In less than thirty seconds, he'd gone through a complete transformation.

Grace's eyes bulged as a hand shot to her mouth. She didn't utter a single word, just shook her head as if she refused to accept what was right in front of her eyes, and then she ran out the door.

Jagger slammed the door to his apartment shut. "I can't believe we lost them!" How had that happened? He'd been hot on that fucker's tail, swerving in and out of traffic with ease. Then the Lincoln had straight up disappeared. "We need to find out everything we can about this fucker. And how he got to Grace?"

"You said you recognized him, right? Was there something you noticed or saw? How did you identify him as a shapeshifter?" his comrade Laurent asked.

Even a skilled hunter like him couldn't typically identify a shapeshifter in their human form. Nothing about them stood out. That wasn't the case with this male. The corner of his lip curled as his eyes narrowed. "Its stench." He'd never forget that smell or that piece of shit had gotten away from him eleven years ago.

Jagger stared at the shifter on the ground before him. A slow grin tugged at the corners of his lips as he watched his prey gasp for air. It wouldn't be long now. He crouched down on his haunches and yanked his blade from the creature's gut. Dragging the knife across his black leather pants, he wiped away the thing's blood and snickered. "Don't worry. Your friend may have gotten away, but I'll find them. Eventually, you all get what you deserve."

When he had come upon the clearing, there had been two of them.

If he hadn't been him, they might have appeared as nothing more than extraordinarily gigantic wolves, but he knew better. He had recognized both creatures for what they were: shifters. The light-colored shifter escaped while he and the light brown shifter fought. But one day, he'd find that piece of shit and end its worthless life.

The creature on the ground took its last breath and its champagne-colored eyes rolled in the back of its head. As its heart stopped pumping, the thing's light brown fur disappeared, its bones rearranged, and a naked woman formed where a wolf once lay.

Hmm, this is a first. Jagger tilted his head. Of all the shifters he'd killed, none had ever been female, that he recalled. Did that mean the other one had been male? Maybe even a pup still. It had looked a little on the young side. Not that he could say for sure. Not that it mattered. He only cared that he had taken the life of one and not two.

That reminded him. He tucked his blade into the sheath at his right hip. Leaning over, Jagger grabbed the sides of the female's face and twisted hard. Shifters had a nasty tendency to heal from their wounds. This way, he ensured the creature was, in fact, dead.

He rose to his full six-foot-one-inch height and dragged a hand through his jet-black hair. Lifting his gaze from his handiwork, Jagger glanced out over the clearing and to the forest beyond it. "One more down. Hundreds more to go."

Champagne eyes. He'd seen eyes that color before. Jagger stalked across the living room, stopped in front of the tall bookcase, and plucked the picture of Grace he kept on a shelf. He traced his finger along one side of her face, staring at those sparkling eyes of hers. It wasn't possible. Except… she'd kissed that *thing*. It all made perfect sense. A low rumble resounded in his chest. Another shifter, right under his fucking nose. For over a year. "She's its mate." Jagger chucked the frame across the room. It smacked into the wall, shattering the glass, and scattered along the floor in pieces.

"Wait… what? I don't get it. What are you talking about?"

"Grace," he snapped. How could he make it any clearer? This entire time, she'd escaped his notice. That was no longer the case.

"No," Laurent retorted. "I refuse to believe you didn't know. You're Jagger Vautour, the finest hunter in all of New York. You've bagged hundreds of shifters, laid down multiple vampires, and protected thousands of people from harm. Women fawn over you. Men wish they could be you. No way you spoke to her several times a week and failed to see it."

His eyebrows knitted together as he folded his arms across his chest. The male had a point. Grace couldn't have fooled him. "Then I guess we'll just have to find out." He had a wicked glint in his eye. The perfect idea popped into his mind. One that would accomplish everything he needed. "And I know just what to do."

CHAPTER *eight*

"GOOD MORNING, SIR," his assistant, Louis, said.

Oh, it was definitely morning. Vincent took another sip of his coffee. It had been a long, eventful night. After Grace had left his house, it had been painful to sit back and watch her get on a bus in a zombie-like state. But he'd followed her until she returned home. Although she'd left her bag at his place, he'd sat hidden in the shadows across the street as she used a spare key to get in. Once he'd been positive, she was inside the house safely, he'd gone back and retrieved her purse.

He hadn't wanted to disturb her, so he'd accessed her house with her own keys and deposited the purse in her kitchen before letting himself out and locking up with the spare key. He would've given anything to comfort her in her time of need. She had gotten a lot of information dumped on her shoulders, but space seemed the better option.

Then he'd gone off and patrolled various parts of the city, seeking that hunter. All he ended up with were a couple of scrapes and bruises, which had already healed, and an overwhelming scent of maple in his nostrils. He'd gone home, washed the sap from his hair and cleaned up. By the time he'd done that, he had two hours to rest before work started.

Swallowing a bit more of his coffee, he nodded to Louis. Yep, it was morning all right. "Morning. Can you do a couple of things for me?"

Taken aback, Louis blinked. He appeared momentarily stunned by the request but quickly collected himself. "Yes, of course, sir. Anything you need."

His assistant's reaction shouldn't have surprised him. The man had been with him for years. When he'd become an editor for the company, he'd decided it was best if his assistant was kin. Back then, he'd still patrolled. Last night was the first time he'd gone out since he stopped nearly ten years back. Vincent scrubbed a hand down his face. "Thank you. Find out everything you can on a Jagger Vautour. And get Chip Descoteaux on the line for me, please."

Louis's eyes widened as he nodded.

Either he was exhausted, or he'd shocked his assistant. If it was the latter, he had no clue what he'd done. Frowning, Vincent headed into his office and dug out his cell phone. He checked his text messages. He hadn't tried calling Grace yet, but he had sent her a couple of texts in the hope she'd respond.

Nothing.

Christ. What did he expect? Not only had he blurted out the truth about her mother, but he'd shifted in front of her. Though there hadn't been another way to get her to see the truth.

Finishing his cup of coffee, he sat in his chair and booted up his computer. How many meetings did he have today? How long before he could go home and sleep a little?

"I have Mr. Descoteaux on the line for you," Louis stated over the intercom.

"Thank you." Vincent picked up the line and opened his mouth—

"What the hell did you do to her now?" Chip asked before he could get out a single word.

Yeah, because it was all automatically his fault. Not Maddie's fault for keeping their world a secret from Grace. Or Chip's fault for not revealing the truth to her sooner. Blame him. The guy left to pick up the pieces. Vincent growled. "I did nothing but tell her the truth. Did you know she has a fucking hunter in her life?"

"What?" The single question came out on a gasp.

"Yeah, smart ass. She has a hunter who has been to the store several times over the last year." Vincent rubbed his eyes. Damn it. Maddie had been a great alpha, but of all the things she could've decided… why keep the truth from Grace? Why not tell the pack about Grace? What did it accomplish? Except endanger Grace's life.

"That's not possible. I've… no… I couldn't have… damn it! Who is it?"

Vincent smirked. He could understand the shock of the situation. Discovering a hunter in Grace's life hadn't pleased him, either. "Jagger Vautour."

"Son of a bitch." Chip groaned. "I always thought it was irresponsible not teaching her how to at least identify hunters, but I believed in her mother's decision."

Leaning back in his chair, Vincent sighed. He could count on his fingers the number of times his former alpha had made a few miscalculations. But any time it had happened, not all the facts had been known. There had to be something she knew about Grace that they didn't. "Maddie had a way of convincing people, even when she was wrong. What exactly did she tell you about Grace?"

"She…" Chip's response trailed off. "Wait, a second. How do you know her mother's name?"

The question caught him off guard. He should've expected it, but he hadn't. His mind wasn't as sharp as usual, likely because of lack of sleep. Or it could be his ever-growing concern for Grace. The one woman who, in an instant, changed everything he ever expected for his life. "I was in her pack."

"Holy fucking shit."

"Yeah." He completely understood the sentiment. Seeing Maddie in a picture with his intended mate had been a shock, especially since he knew more about the details regarding her death than most. Save for the one who caused it. Vincent rubbed his eyes. They were getting off point here. "Back to my last question. What exactly did she tell you about Grace?" He had to gain control of the situation with Grace, which started with finding that damn hunter.

Chip was silent for a minute. "When she made me her ward, she said that Grace could change the future and how we dealt with hunters. I pushed for details, but she said nothing more on the matter. All I can say for sure is that whatever she knew about Grace… it worried her."

Change the future? Was it possible Grace had some sixth sense? She'd spaced out that one time in the store. He hadn't known what to make of it. Maybe this was the clue he'd been missing. "We don't have time to figure it all out. Grace knows the truth, and she didn't handle it well."

"Please don't tell me you fought the hunter in front of her."

"Not in the way you think." He hadn't gone full fledge wolf until much later in the evening. None of which he'd planned for. His intention had been a discussion, a night of questions, answers, and love making. It didn't go down that way at all.

"What'd you do? Wolf out on her?" Sarcasm dripped with his words.

Vincent opened his mouth and snapped it shut. The simple answer: yes. Long and drawn-out answer: she didn't want to believe, so he proved her wrong.

"Oh, hell. You couldn't make any of this easy, could you?"

"We can spend the next hour going into the logistics, but that won't resolve anything." They were all to blame. That was the bottom line of the situation. Maddie had decided without sharing all the reasons with anyone. Chip had blindly followed her instructions. And him? He'd gone into everything half-assed, only thinking about the impact to himself and no one else, not even Grace.

"Fine. We have a standing lunch, so I'll talk to her."

"Thank you." The words felt foreign in his mouth. Maybe that was why his assistant had looked at him funny. He'd somehow located his manners.

Grace took the seat across from Chip. She set the salad on his desk and took a bite from her bacon-cheeseburger. He was her best friend. Of all the people she knew, he should be the one person she could tell about last night. He'd understand, right?

Not that she had any idea where to begin. Or if she could even explain. She was still processing it all herself. *Shapeshifters are real.* Grace swallowed the food in her mouth and lifted her cup of Coke to her mouth. How was she supposed to tell him that without sounding like a lunatic?

Chip pushed some leaves of his salad around with his fork. "You're awfully quiet today."

"I have a lot on my mind." And she didn't know how to talk to him about any of it. She'd been useless in her classes. She'd spent most of the morning sorting through her memories with her mother, looking for clues. Some sign she'd missed.

She discovered a lot of them. The house always smelled like Maplewood. Her mother's late-night runs. Or the number of hours she'd been away from the house. The times her mother returned home looking like she'd been in a brawl, only to appear untouched the next day.

The time in the park—they'd been coming back from a picnic and her mother forced her to hide. Her mother had disappeared for almost an hour, but she'd been right where her mother had left her. She remembered the sinking feeling she had in her belly that day. Back then, she thought it had to have resulted from believing she'd gotten left behind. What if it there was more to it?

Grace blinked.

Chip didn't sit behind his desk any longer. He'd moved to the chair to her left.

When had that happened? Fuck, she'd zoned out again. Graced buried her face in her hands.

"I will have none of that." Chip tugged at her arm until her eyes met his.

She stared into his hazel gaze. Her lips pressed together as she ran a hand through her caramel-colored hair. She wanted to tell him, but she didn't want to sound crazy either. Grace groaned and slumped in the chair. "I just don't know what to do."

"Maybe I can help with that, but before I explain, I need you to promise you won't get mad at me."

Mad at him? Why would she—Grace perked up a bit. Did he know? Was he a part of that world, too? She glanced over her shoulder and noticed the door had shut. Leaning in a little closer, Grace whispered, "Are you a shapeshifter, too?"

Chip burst out in laughter. He bent over and gripped his knees as his chuckling echoed around the office.

Leaning back in the chair, Grace frowned. She crossed her arms and glared at him. She didn't think it was that funny. It had been a rather serious question. "It's nice to know I can amuse you."

He settled with a grin. "I'm sorry. I've gotten accused of a lot of things, but never of a shapeshifter. No, Grace, I'm kin, like you."

"What?" She didn't just hear that. No absolutely-fucking-way had he kept this from her. It didn't happen.

Lacing his fingers together behind his head, he nodded. "My father is a shapeshifter, my mother's human. I'm kin, the same as you are."

"Are you fucking kidding me?" She jumped to her feet. He was supposed to be her best friend, and he outright admitted to knowing about a world she was supposedly a part of. "Is this some kind of sick joke?"

His smile faltered as he sat ramrod straight in the rose-toned chair. "I would never lie about anything like this."

"You just didn't bother telling me. You've been my best friend for fifteen years and you've kept this a secret the whole time." She really had no reason to be so indignant with him. Not when she had her own secret—one she hadn't ever shared. But this was different. This was a world she should've grown up knowing about. Instead, he'd decided not to tell her anything. Who else in her life had done it? Her mother? Her father?

Chip ran a hand through his brown hair and leaned forward on his knees. "I'm sorry, Grace. It's what your mother wanted. I followed her requests to watch over you and keep you protected from the truth."

Grace paced from one side of the office to the other as she chewed on the inside of her cheek. Her mother had done everything for her safety. Wouldn't it make sense that the more she knew about her own world, the safer she would be? Then why would her mother do everything in her power to keep this from her? It made little sense. "If that's the case, then why tell me now?"

His Adam's apple bobbed as he swallowed and flicked his gaze to a side wall. "I went to Vincent's office the other day and told him to back off. As your ward—" Chip held up a hand to stop her from asking questions. "I promise, I'll explain. As your ward, it's my responsibility to ensure your safety. That includes checking out every guy you date or even talk to. Our laws govern the way potential mates should approach you."

Mate? Ward? Who the hell used words like that? She didn't. She typically called them boyfriends. This was something else entirely. Seeing Vincent change the way he had last night… it freaked her out. She hadn't been able to handle it.

There Chip sat, adding more to all she'd felt, all she was still feeling… how much more was a girl supposed to take? Grace slowly sat down in the chair. "So, you've what? Run background checks on all the men I've dated before?"

"Something to that effect. I mean, I can't legally run background checks on them, but I've followed them, spoken with their friends, had a P.I. investigate one or two."

"Including Gabriel?" A private investigator? What friend hired—oh wait, that's right, he wasn't her friend. He was her *ward*, whatever the fuck that meant. She got back to her feet once again and paced from one side of the office to the other.

Did shapeshifter laws revert to the 1950s with women? No. That couldn't be the case. Chip said he *checked* her exes out, but not once had he ever interfered in a relationship. Except he had. He was the one who had pointed out Vincent's true identity. He had gone to Vincent's office—a place she hadn't even been yet.

"I found out he was a drug dealer fairly early on. He was a horrible man, but I didn't want to decide for you, so I hired a bodyguard to monitor you. If something had even started to go awry, he would've snatched you up on the spot."

That didn't make her feel better. It had taken her months to find that out and end the relationship. Why was Vincent different? Aside from the obvious—he was a shapeshifter—she had a much stronger attraction to him than anyone else, and his bright, electric-blue eyes, that strong jawline of his, the way his biceps bulged when he held her close, and how perfectly she fit into his arms all added to that.

But it was more than physical. Everything with Vincent was different. Like nothing she'd ever experienced before. Her emotions were completely out of whack. Grace sighed. "Then why talk to Vincent? Why interfere with our relationship when you didn't with any of my others?"

Chip looked her straight in the eyes. "Because he has the potential to be permanent. That changes your life drastically."

Vincent… a permanent fixture? Her eyes widened as she stopped in the middle of the room and slowly sat back down. Grace swallowed to wet her parched throat. She could imagine spending the rest of her life with him.

How was that even possible? They'd known one another all of a week. Gone on… three, maybe four dates. Spent half that time arguing and pushing each other's buttons.

One statement broke through all the noise in her head. *"You feel like home."*

He had a point. He felt like home, too.

Jagger scanned the living room of Grace's apartment. How had she lived so close to the shop all this time without his knowledge? He'd visited her so much over the last year. Not once had he ever learned where she lived. He strode around the plush couch, running his fingers along the exquisitely soft armrest as he eyed the various pictures hung above the television. Nothing stood out. A photograph of Grace and her father hung amongst them, along with a few others of Grace and friends, or so he assumed.

His gaze landed on a gilded picture frame that sat to the left of the television. It contained a photograph of a female with brown hair, champagne-colored eyes, and high cheekbones along with a child of similar features. Same bright champagne eyes, long, caramel-brown hair, and oval-shaped face as Grace. Plucking the frame from its location, Jagger studied it. Yes, this was definitely Grace, perhaps around age ten, sitting with the older female at a picnic. His eyes narrowed as his jaw clenched. "Son of a bitch."

The whore he'd killed eleven years ago was her mother. Roaring, he chucked the picture across the room. Heaving ragged breaths, Jagger knocked the television onto the floor. It crashed onto the ground, shards of glass cracking. The picture hadn't proven Grace was a shapeshifter, but it had shown him what he needed to know. He glowered at Laurent, who hovered nearby. "Destroy everything. She's just as evil as those filthy monsters."

Though he didn't plan to stick around, he'd make damn sure she knew what happened. Preparations had to be made. Weapons had to be collected. Once he had all the arrangements in place, he'd come back.

This was far from over.

Her lunch with Chip had gone longer than normal, which was fine. Until she realized her father had known the truth all along as well. While it cleared up his initial reaction to Vincent, it added more to her questions.

Instead of going to work, she'd called her father and demanded he close the store early so they could talk. Boy, did they talk. Grace groaned. She'd spent almost four hours discussing, along with a little arguing, everything with her father.

The plus side was she'd learned more about her mother in the last twenty-four hours than she had in the first ten years of her life.

Now, all she wanted to do was go home, have a glass of wine, and mull over… her life. Fuck, it had taken a turn she'd never expected. Taking her house keys out of her pocket, Grace started up the staircase. She paused halfway into her ascent.

The welcome mat in front of her apartment sat at an angle. Her front door appeared to be open. She hadn't left it that way. She dug around in her purse for the pepper spray her father insisted she carry.

Grace finished the trek up the stairs to her apartment. Her door wasn't open. It was on the ground. Someone had ripped it off its hinges. With a brief swallow, she steeled her shoulders, eased her backpack to the floor, and readied the pepper spray.

She didn't know what she was going to find, but at least she came prepared. Wiping the sweat from her clammy hands, she stepped over the broken door and tiptoed into the foyer. She scanned the living room and kitchen—there wasn't anyone there, but it had all gotten trashed.

Someone had torn apart and thrown all of her Christmas decorations on the floor. They had dragged a blade through every cushion on the couch, all the stuffing strewn about the floor. They'd yanked the television from the stand and tossed it on the ground. The glass in the pictures of her and her mother lay scattered in pieces across the hardwood floor. At least half of her dishes, plates, and glassware had all gotten chucked aside. Glass shards littered the kitchen tile.

Swallowing again, she ambled down the hallway as quietly as she'd entered her place. Grace paused in front of her bathroom. They'd shattered the mirror and strewn all her personal items across the bathroom. Why would someone do this?

Shaking away the growing sense of panic in her racing heart, she trudged forward into her bedroom. It was more of the same, with a few differences. Her shredded clothes lay everywhere, while family pictures had gotten cracked and ripped apart all over the place.

That's where the similarities ended. The petals she'd saved from the two roses Vincent had given her were in a complete disarray atop the torn-apart bed. Someone had stabbed a blade through the only picture she had of her and Vincent into the wall over her bed. Above that, they'd scrawled two words in red spray paint.

Die, bitch.

Grace removed her cell phone from her back pocket and accessed her contact list. She couldn't call the police. With all she had learned, this wasn't a typical break-in. Who did she call?

Not Chip. As her ward, she didn't know what he *could* do. He'd flip a lid and likely go into a protective mode she hadn't seen yet.

Not her father. His overbearing nature wasn't any better. She'd be lucky if he let her continue working in the shop.

It only left one person. Biting the inside of her lip, Grace scrolled to J. Even after she'd learned his full name, his real one, she hadn't changed it in her phone.

She listened to Vincent's line ring once before he picked up.

"Grace, I'm—"

"I need help." She refused to waste time. The intruder might've waited nearby for her to return home. All she had to defend herself was pepper spray.

The tone in his voice changed. "Are you okay? What's going on?"

"Someone broke into my apartment."

"I'm on my way."

CHAPTER *nine*

"GRACE?" A MALE voice called from around the corner of what remained of her front door.

She stood there with her hand outstretched, one finger on the pepper spray's release button in case she needed to use it. "Who are you?"

A pair of calloused hands came into view. "I'm Derek, a friend of Vincent's. He sent me to get a new door up for you."

"Where's Vincent?" Grace bounced back and forth on the balls of her feet. He'd stayed with her on the phone for a few minutes, but he had mentioned nothing about sending anyone.

"He's…" the man's words trailed off. A set of two voices exchanged a brief greeting, followed by a few things she couldn't make out.

"I'm right here, Grace." Vincent stepped in front of the entryway and into her line of sight.

With a sigh of relief, she dropped the canister of pepper spray on the floor, darted across the door, and launched herself into his arms.

He easily caught her, hugging her tight against his body as he carried her back into the apartment.

Tears streamed down her cheeks as she held onto him. A half hour ago, she'd been ready to spend the next day deciding what all the new information she'd heard meant for them. She'd been ready to let him go… if it came to that. Instead, she stepped into her apartment and all of that changed.

"Hey, you're okay." Vincent strode into the kitchen with her legs wrapped around his waist. He set her down on the one thing that had been untouched—the countertop. Tucking a strand of her hair back, he pressed a tender kiss to her forehead and wiped away her tears. "I've got you."

"I don't understand why someone would do this." It was supposed to be a safe neighborhood, a quiet neighborhood, one where most people got along. Nothing about this was quiet or safe. It was angry and vengeful.

"We'll do a walkthrough in a second and figure that out. Right now, I'm going to go talk to Derek and see about a new door for you. Just stay here." He leaned down and brushed a chaste kiss across her lips. "I promise I'll be right back."

Inhaling a deep breath, Grace nodded. She bit her bottom lip as he walked around to the door where the other man waited. Most of the broken dishes had been contained to the floor in front of the sink. She released the breath she'd held and hopped down from the counter. Sitting up there made her feel more like a child than a grown woman.

She glanced over her shoulder and eyed the man Vincent spoke with. Derek, as he'd called himself, had perfectly coiffed midnight black hair and wide steel-blue eyes. The man stood a couple of inches shorter than Vincent, but he was slightly bulkier in build. It was obvious his job was a manual labor of some kind.

"Okay, thank you." Vincent clapped Derek on the back and strode over to the kitchen.

"How do you know him?" The two of them had addressed one another as old friends in almost the same manner she and Chip talked, which wasn't something she'd ever seen in Vincent before.

Vincent held his hand out to her. "He's a former pack member."

That's right. Chip had told her Vincent's pack had ostracized him, but he refused to go into further detail. After the conversation they had about her mother, it had been enough to satisfy her curiosity. Although, apparently, not all of them turned their backs on Vincent. She settled her hand in his.

"Show me the major part of this."

Right. Her room. She led him down the hall to her bedroom, where she'd ascertained the attack was personal. To both of them.

Seeing Grace so small and vulnerable made his blood boil. If he hadn't planned on killing that hunter before, he sure as hell did now. Both he and Derek had picked up on the moss scent at the bottom of the staircase. It was all over the apartment.

None of the damage had been minimal, but at least it could all be repaired or replaced. Nothing had happened to Grace. That had been more important than the broken items.

Fixing the door would take a bit of work, but Derek assured him he could handle it. He'd been the only pack member that still spoke to him. They didn't hang out, but they'd stayed in touch.

Vincent walked with Grace back to her bedroom, their fingers threaded together as they ambled down the hall. He noted the minor damage inflicted on the bathroom. The mirror had taken the brunt of it. As they stepped into the bedroom, his eyes immediately flicked to the two words spray-painted above the bed, then they shifted to the picture of them stabbed to the wall directly below.

If nothing else had convinced him before, he certainly believed it now. Jagger had ransacked Grace's apartment and left a blatant threat on her wall. His gaze fell to the wilted rose petals across the bed. "What's that?"

"Those? Oh, they're the petals from the roses you gave me."

"You kept those?" He glanced over at her. That hadn't been something he'd expected to hear. He always presumed she'd toss them once they died, but for her to keep the petals… his lips tugged into a small smile.

"Of course, I did. I would not throw them in the trash. They deserved better treatment than that."

"That's really thoughtful." His eyes shot back to the words on the wall and the picture. Jagger had it out for both of them. He'd continue his nightly patrols, but until he located the hunter, he couldn't risk Grace's life.

"Do you think it's a coincidence?" Grace asked.

"No."

Her shoulders heaved with a heavy sigh. "I was afraid you'd say that."

"I'm sorry someone targeted you like this." Vincent opened his mouth to say more and snapped it shut. She wasn't just a random piece of bait for some hunter to use against a shapeshifter. Grace was the daughter of a shapeshifter, one who'd gotten killed, as well as involved with him. This wouldn't likely be the first time a hunter would take a shot at her.

Grace narrowed her champagne orbs at him and scowled. "I think you mean *us.* Whoever did this didn't just come for me, they came for both of us, you and me, together."

He had no argument against the truth. Jagger had aimed for the two of them. The buzzing sound of a drill came from the front room and overrode anything he considered offering as comfort.

Glancing over her shoulders, Grace wrapped an arm around his waist. "Even with a new door, I can't stay here. Everything… all my furniture will have to be replaced. I can't do that while my father's working. He'd freak out if he saw this."

"You'll stay with me. In the meantime, Derek will have a crew work at night to address the wreckage." It was one of the first things they'd discussed as they assessed the damage to the front door. The man had given him a cockeyed look. None of his pack members had known him for taking women to his home. Little did the guy know Grace had already been there.

"You'd do that?"

Without hesitation. He couldn't fathom a life without her. The door would only do so much to keep her safe. He was much better at protection.

Vincent tilted his head and offered her a small smile. "It's a little self-serving, but I'd do anything to protect you."

"I meant work with your former pack member, even if it is just to help me."

He pursed his lips. He hadn't mentioned why Derek was a former pack member. Something about the way her features softened and how her eyebrows drew together indicated a bit of understanding and compassion. Maybe she didn't know everything that happened, but someone had told her enough. Vincent cupped her cheek. Leaning his forehead against hers, he inhaled her sweet honey scent. "Don't you know that I'd do anything for you?"

Standing on her tiptoes, her lips fused with his. Her tongue swept the inside of his mouth as the kiss deepened. A strong need grew between the two of them, almost as if their souls couldn't survive without the other.

Sliding his hands down her back, he gripped her ass and gave it a quick squeeze. He swallowed the moan that escaped her lips. If they weren't wading through a mountain of destruction and if Derek hadn't been working in the foyer… the things he'd do to her. Vincent released the kiss.

Grace's cheeks flushed with heat. She bit her bottom lip as a challenge sparkled in her champagne-colored eyes.

A low growl rumbled from his throat. "Pack some clothes while I collect your personal items from the bathroom and check on Derek's progress."

Nipping his top lip, she waggled her eyebrows and sauntered past him. Her teasing tone didn't last. Her gaze swept over the pile of shredded clothes. She bent over and scooped one of her blouses from the floor. "I just can't fathom who would do this."

Vincent scrubbed his face and dropped his hands to his hips. "It's Jagger. If you look at what he's done, along with his actions yesterday… it makes sense."

"You really think it's Jagger?" Grace peered at him over her shoulder.

"I know it is. I can smell him all over your apartment." He didn't have to explain that further. Vincent gestured to her closet. "Get some clothes packed. I'll be right back."

The drive to Vincent's place had been in silence. He carried her small bag of luggage inside.

The truth that Jagger had destroyed her sanctuary had been a hard pill to swallow. She'd known he'd be the jealous type, but she didn't think he'd ever go so far to destroy her… them. None of what the man had done had been about her alone. He'd aimed for both her and Vincent. Was this what she had to look forward to in a relationship with a shapeshifter? Hunters after them constantly.

What if they had kids?

Maybe that's why her mother refused to share anything about the shapeshifter world. It wasn't much, but it made sense. Parents did whatever they could to protect their children. Was it enough to steer her away from Vincent?

As if she'd spoken his name out loud, he glimpsed at her. "Why don't I draw a bath for you?"

"That sounds nice. Thank you." She watched as he disappeared down the hallway toward his bedroom with her luggage still in hand. No. It wasn't.

Even with the memory of him in his large wolf form, she couldn't see herself with anyone else. In such a short time, he'd barged into her heart and set up shop. That meant they'd have to deal with Jagger.

They could do that, though. She didn't know if she could take another life, but maybe there was another option. One she didn't know about yet. She still knew so little of their world.

"Hey. Bath's ready." Vincent stroked her cheek with the back of his knuckles.

Grace gasped, startled by the tender movement. She hadn't seen or heard him return. "Sorry. I guess I was… sorry."

"You don't have to apologize to me. The last couple of days haven't been the easiest."

No, they hadn't. No way she'd argue against that, but they all brought her here. Standing in front of a gorgeous man whom she cared for deeply. A tiny smile crossed her lips. "Not the least bit."

Taking her hand in his own, he squeezed it and nodded toward the bathroom. "I've got a nice hot bath for you. It should help."

Her gaze swept over his face as she bit her bottom lip. He was tall. Was the tub big enough for both of them? If it was, maybe she could distract them both from everything going on around them. She wouldn't mind stealing a moment for just the two of them. "Will you join me?"

"I can." Vincent turned them in the direction of the bathroom and led the way.

Grace stopped in the bathroom's doorway; her eyes widened as she drank in the sight. It was nothing like what she'd described in her manuscript. To her left was a double-sink crystal blue granite counter with a large mirror hung above it. Between that and the toilet sat a wooden cabinet. On the opposite side of the room was a shower, big enough for two people. To her right, a large white jacuzzi tub. The star and moon patterned tile pulled it all together. "When did this happen?"

"When did what happen?"

"This." She gestured toward the tub and expansion of the bathroom.

Vincent tugged her further inside. "A few years ago. I wanted something a little more updated."

Her mouth formed a silent *oh*. At least it was one thing that had gotten changed before she'd written her manuscript. Good to know.

They both quickly shed their clothes. Vincent climbed into the tub first and extended a hand to help her in. Easing into the water, he sat on the bench.

She stood there, fully naked, with water up to the apex of her thighs. Hot blood rolling through her veins and he didn't look at all interested. Maybe he needed a little convincing.

Grace straddled him. The water sluicing against her breasts. She ran her wet fingers through his hair and brushed a kiss across his lips. Her tongue swept across his lower lip as she gently plied his mouth open. Once he opened up, she deepened the kiss and softly gripped the nape of his neck.

His hands ran up her thighs and his arms wrapped around the small of her back. The jets in the tub kicked on. Vincent stroked the back of her head and released the kiss.

"Don't stop, please." Her eyes met his. Unshed tears prickled the corners of her eyes. Damn it, her emotions bubbled to the surface. It was exactly what she planned to avoid. "I don't want to think about what's on the other side waiting for us."

"Are you sure?"

Yes. No. She didn't know if making love to him right then would absolve her residual anger. She didn't know if it would offer any more insight into how they could make this work. What she knew… she needed to feel connected to him. To break the barrier that had made its way between them. This would do that. Everything else, they could figure out afterward. "Yes. I need you. We need this."

Her last words were his undoing. His lips fused with hers as his hand fisted her hair and pulled her closer to his body.

Her breasts pressed into his chest. The heat of his wet skin sent shivers down her spine. She moaned into the deepened kiss and tightened her hold on to the nape of his neck.

She felt his erection up against her slit and ass. Shifting slightly, Grace dug her nails into Vincent's shoulder blades and gyrated against him. The head of his cock rubbed against the seams of her sex and pulled another moan from her.

The water sloshed around them. His fingers skimmed across her leg and made their way to the apex of her thighs. Vincent slipped one digit inside her and then another.

Her head fell back with a groan as her back arched. She rocked against his fingers. Electricity vibrated through her body as his fingers moved deep inside of her.

A growl rumbled in the back of his throat as a heated gaze fell across his face. His mouth trailed along her jawline, down her neck to her collarbone. He nipped at one of her nipples, latched onto her breast as he added his thumb to the mix and rubbed her clit.

Her belly tensed as an orgasm ripped through her body. The inner walls of her core pulsated around Vincent's fingers as she rode the sensations coursing through her veins.

Lifting his head from her breast, he removed his fingers, gripped her hips, and thrust his cock deep inside her core.

They both cried out in ecstasy.

Her walls were tight around his thick girth.

Entangling a hand in her hair, his lips crashed against hers. His tongue penetrated her mouth as his cock pistoned in and out of her, repeatedly. The combined force of their bodies coming together as one quickly spiraling out of control.

Fire raced through her body and lit every one of her synapses, taking her to the edge. Grace ground against him as Vincent met her stroke for stroke. Each one taking her higher than the last.

Breaking off the kiss, Vincent grabbed a hold of her hips again and pounded into her as if she were his lifeline.

Both of their bodies were slick with sweat. The water splashed around them.

His fingers dug into her skin as his hold tightened. His electric-blue eyes were glassy with uncontrollable need as he continued to drive into her deep.

Grace dragged her nails across his shoulder blades and gripped onto his shoulders as another orgasm barreled through her body, sending Vincent right into his own. The two of them rode the sensations out until the last shudder.

Breathing raggedly, she dropped her head into the crook of his neck. That had been exactly what they both needed. She could tell by the way his fingers skimmed up and down her back.

"I thought the purpose of this bath was to relax," Vincent said after a moment.

Catching her breath, she smiled. "I found it very relaxing. In fact, I feel like butter. I think you accomplished your task."

He pressed a loving kiss to her forehead and wrapped her up in his arms. "It wasn't how I thought it'd happen, but I'm glad."

"I think you did a wonderful job." Grace kissed his chest softly and looked up at him. Yeah, she could see waking up to him every morning, having more moments like this where they held one another in the afterglow.

"Right back at you." Cupping her chin, Vincent brushed a tender kiss across her lips. "Now that we're good and dirty, what do you say we get cleaned up?"

"I think that sounds like a plan."

They spent the next ten minutes using the body wash she'd packed to suds one another up, then rinsed off. Just as Vincent helped her into the tub, he helped her out.

It wasn't until they were standing in the middle of the bathroom drying off that she noticed it. First, on her own skin. Grace flicked her eyes to him. And then eyed his flesh.

Her eyes widened as she looked Vincent over from head to toe and drank in the sight of the glimmer of his skin. She glanced over her shoulder and back at him. Stifling a laugh, Grace hooked a thumb at the tub. "Did you put something in the water?"

"Yeah. One of the bath bombs you had at your place. Why?"

Covering her mouth with her hand, she pointed to his skin and wiggled her eyebrows. If she dared utter a word, she wouldn't be able to stop what followed.

Vincent looked down at himself. "What the fuck?"

Her boyfriend was sparkling. Unable to contain herself any longer, she doubled over in laughter.

"This isn't funny, Grace. I'm shining like a fucking star."

His words started her laughter all over again. She clutched at him for support. He was shiny, in the worst way possible. His olive skin tone twinkled with glitter. Grace caught her breath. A wide grin settled on her face. "You're sparkles."

"What? Oh, no. You're not giving me a nickname out of this. It was *your* bath bomb. Besides, you're just as shiny as I am."

"I know, but you're the shapeshifter." She chuckled again. It really shouldn't have amused her so much. All she could see was the glitter in his hair. She didn't entirely know how it worked, but with it covering his body like that… did that mean it would show up in his fur?

"Oh, hell." As if the full meaning of her statement hit him, Vincent turned and checked his reflection in the mirror.

"Sparkles," she said with a giggle.

"I'm going to show you sparkles." He spun on his heel, scooped her up, and tossed her over his shoulder. He swatted her ass.

Grace squealed as he carried her across the hall to his bedroom.

CHAPTER Ten

LEAVING GRACE ALONE at his place hadn't been optimal, but he had little choice. She had schoolwork, and he didn't fancy bringing her along to meet his former pack.

His short time last night with Derek reminded him that there might be people willing to help. If not for him, then for Maddie. The woman may be gone, but they all respected her enough to help him protect Grace.

He needed help to find this hunter.

And thanks to Derek, he knew just where to find his pack. Vincent opened the door to Penelope's and stepped inside the country-chic restaurant. It wasn't huge, like some of the fancier restaurants he usually ate at, but it was homey. The bar was at the back, the breakfast counter to the right, and the wooden tables to the left.

His nose found the group of large men before his eyes. Their unique scents permeated his nostrils. He headed straight for the group sitting at a table at the back of the restaurant. Best seat in the house—where they could watch every entryway and exit.

Upon his approach, Phillip's gaze met his. "What the hell are you doing here?"

The male had always been straight to the point. Vincent swallowed. He'd never required aid from anyone. There was a first time for everything. "I need your help."

"Like we'd help you." Phillip scoffed.

Vincent pinched the bridge of his nose. Going in, he knew this wouldn't be easy, but he didn't think they'd be outright defiant. He dropped his hands to his waist. "Can you please hear me out first?"

"Why? So, you can get one of us killed next?" Lucian tossed out.

He'd been a coward and ill-experienced, but he hadn't been responsible for Maddie's death. Not that it stopped the pack from blaming him. He'd been there when they'd come across the hunter. He should've never left her to fight the hunter alone, but she'd insisted. Vincent growled. "I'm not the same boy I was back then, so don't for one second think you can bully me."

"Come on, guys. It's been over ten years. Can't we let this go?" Leave it to Derek, the reasonable one, to come through on his behalf.

"He got our alpha killed." Amir hissed, his voice low enough none of the restaurant occupants could hear their conversation.

"I didn't get her killed, but I didn't stay when I should have." If he'd stayed back then, the two of them together could've taken the hunter out. Maybe. Or at least stalled him until the rest of the pack had arrived. No matter what, the entire situation had to be handled with care. He couldn't afford to lose his cool and blow up at any of them.

"Not a single one of us knows what happened that night. Who's saying the outcome would be different if any of us had been in Vincent's place?" Ethan's gaze shifted from one pack member to the next.

He didn't recall the guy speaking up much in the past. In fact, the two of them had always been the quietest. They were both the same age. Maybe Ethan had grown as much as he had over the years.

Amir crossed his arms and glanced at Phillip. "Alpha? The decision's yours."

Obviously, the dynamics of the pack had changed. A new alpha had to be appointed. If the old one died in combat, the pack usually handled it as a vote. Phillip had been beta back then. It made sense they moved him to the alpha. Vincent laced his fingers together as he waited.

"Fine. Take a seat," Phillip said, gesturing to the empty chair.

"Thank you." He sat down in the unoccupied wooden chair and glanced around at his old pack. A week ago, he would've never considered sitting amongst these men again. They'd betrayed him. None of them had been willing to hear him out back then. Every one of them blamed him for Maddie's death because he left.

They'd labeled him a coward and ostracized him from the community of shapeshifters in the city, including his own pack. No one believed he could be anything more.

Now he sat here, well-versed in human society and out of touch with his own kind. Even patrolling the other night had been more grueling than he remembered. Vincent leaned forward on the table, digging his elbows into the wood, and sighed. "She ordered me to leave."

All five men shouted simultaneously, "What?"

Vincent glared at the men across from him. They didn't need to draw attention to their conversation. Details of the fight itself weren't important. They'd seen his wounds. The most important part had been the brief argument he'd lost to Maddie. "After I got hurt, she sent me away. I tried to fight her on it, but she was the alpha. What was I supposed to do, disregard her order?"

"Yes," Ethan said.

"And how many times have you defied his orders?" Vincent gestured to Phillip. Who did they think they were talking to? The eighteen-year-old boy he'd been back then? The boy who had still been learning how to control his overly-sized body? He wasn't any of that now.

Ethan harrumphed, sat back in his chair and crossed his arms like a petulant child.

"Exactly what I thought."

Phillip held up a hand to silence the others and calm them down. "Okay, but that can't be what brought you to us today."

"You're right. It isn't. The hunter that killed Maddie is still alive... and after her daughter." He didn't add in that Jagger taunted him as well. That was the entire intention behind the stabbed photograph of them. He was certain of it.

"Daughter? What daughter?" Lucian asked.

Gripping the back of his neck, Vincent inwardly groaned. The question didn't shock him. He didn't know about Grace until a few days ago. Why should any of the rest of them have known about her existence? "Maddie has a daughter. She's twenty-one."

Amir snorted. "How is it we're just finding out about this?"

"Because Madelyn was protective of her family," Derek responded.

"And why is it you don't seem surprised by this news?" Phillip raised an eyebrow.

Derek grinned and tossed a glance back at Vincent. "I think I'll let him explain that."

Right. He hadn't yet mentioned Grace was his mate or that he'd been seeing her. Or that he'd reached out to Derek earlier. Vincent scrubbed his face and tensed his shoulders. "He met Grace last night. The hunter, Jagger, ransacked her apartment likely in response to seeing Grace and I together a couple of days ago. It would seem she's my mate."

"Are you fucking kidding me?" Ethan growled and thrust a hand into his fiery red hair. "Out of all of us, you find your intended first? And it isn't some rando, it's Maddie's fucking daughter? This just gets better and better."

None of it had been easy... on either of them. Not that he planned to share that. Vincent opened his mouth—

"What's it like? Meeting your intended mate, I mean," Amir asked, his hazel eyes intently focused on him.

That was a good question. Nothing had worked out right. The first time they met. His approach to a date. Lying about his identity and making it all right. Her father's reaction to him. Finding out who she really was and how little she knew about it. Yet, he wouldn't trade a single moment of it for a different version. "A beautiful mess."

Grace's hand fell away from her chin as she nodded off. Her head snapped back up. *I'm awake.* She glanced around the empty dining room. Right, she wasn't in class. She was studying at Vincent's place. Or attempting to, anyway.

Standing up, she stretched her arms and shook her whole body out. How long had she been at this table? She eyed the time on her watch. It was only eleven. Shit. She'd barely been at the books for two hours. It had to be all the love-making from the night before that left her so exhausted.

Maybe a round of exploration would help wake her up. She had an exam coming at the end of the week. Studying was a must. It was half her grade. Grace left the dining room and poked a little around the kitchen.

She half-paid it any attention the other day. Her gaze caught sight of a couple of different appliances. A toaster oven, microwave, nothing special until her eyes found the double oven. She cooked a little. With an oven like that, did Vincent? If not, she might have a reason to learn.

Everything was a brightly polished silver. Hmm, didn't myths say shapeshifters were highly sensitive to silver? Or was that werewolves? She shrugged. Either way, it had to be wrong. Otherwise, she couldn't see the purpose behind all the silver appliances.

Nothing else about the kitchen piqued her interest, so she continued into the living room across the way. It didn't look any different from a couple of nights ago. Though she hadn't noticed the glass coffee table with the antique metal legs and ornate decoration around the edge. It was a stunning piece. Too bad he'd opted for that instead of his parents' original piece. She'd love to have a unique piece like that in her father's store.

Her gaze shifted to the mantel and empty walls. No portraits of any kind. He had to miss his parents. It would explain why he left everything bare and void of memories. Grace frowned and headed down the hallway. She strolled into the spare bedroom.

It had gotten redecorated in white and teal. The bedspread had a beautiful design of fluttering feathers with matching pillows. To the right was a dark wood dresser to contrast the lighter colors of the bed. In the far corner sat a white lounge chair. She dragged her fingers across the teal blanket laid over the arm.

The room appeared comfortable and welcoming for any guest. She left the spare bedroom and strode next door to Vincent's room. It's where she'd spent the night. Although there was a dark blue starry night comforter on the bed, she'd gotten most of her warmth from Vincent. He was like her own personal heater. The comforter hadn't been necessary. Just like in the spare bedroom, there was a dark wood dresser. Except in here there was a matching desk. And the corner chair was the same blue as the comforter, with a pale-yellow blanket.

But again, no portraits or pictures. Three paintings hung on the walls, but other than that, they were all completely bare. Grace bit the inside of her cheek and poked her head into the hallway.

Before he'd left that morning, Vincent told her all rooms were open to her except the master. Could it be the one place where she might find some memories? If so, why did he keep it locked up? Unless… maybe … she glanced both ways down the hall and tiptoed to the master bedroom.

If it was unlocked, she'd look. If it was locked, she'd let it go. Grace dropped her eyes to the door knob.

Now or never.

She gripped the knob and slowly turned it—unlocked. Glancing over her shoulder one last time, she pushed the door open and eyed the room. Picture frames covered the white antique dresser to the right. Family photographs hung above the king-sized bed. To the left there were shelves upon shelves of photos—two walls full. Her eyes widened as she drank in the sight.

Wow. Vincent must've moved all of his family's photographs into his parents' bedroom. There were so many. She knew his parents had died, but he'd never said how. For him to hide everything like this, their lives must've ended tragically. Unless… could they have died in a car accident as she'd written in her manuscript? Grace swallowed and entered the bedroom.

She started with the pictures on top of the dresser. There wasn't any order to them. They scaled across ages. There was one with his parents on a camping trip. They looked exactly the way she'd described them in her manuscript. Those visions… it explained so much. Her story had been about his family. Vincent seemed so happy. There was another one of him working alongside his father. He had to be maybe ten.

Seeing him next to the man, he'd gotten so much of his father's looks. The same height, same chiseled jaw, but his eyes and dirty-blond hair… those belonged to his mother. Could that be why he'd hidden these? It had been painful for years after her mother's death to see the pictures of their time together, but even if they'd been stored away—it couldn't stop the memories. Those were always with her. Wouldn't it be the same for him?

Grace walked back to the wall closest to the door. More scattered memories of happy times. One caught her attention. Her mother stood with the forest to her back with six other young men, including Vincent. All the men were of varying ages. Vincent appeared to be in his late teens, early twenties. She picked the picture up.

The second her hand touched the frame, her mind's eye opened.

Two massive wolves walked side by side toward a clearing. The male had white fur and electric-blue eyes. His shoulders reached nearly five feet in height. The other wolf, a female, had light-brown fur and champagne-colored eyes. She stood a little over four feet.

"Do you think we'll come across anything?" the male, Vincent, asked.

"It's too early to call it a night, so don't even—" the female, Madelyn, stopped a few feet into the clearing. Her ears prickled.

He paused not far away.

Neither of them moved for a moment. A dark-haired male jumped out from a nearby bush and landed on the white-wolf's back.

Not dodging the landing, he bucked to throw the hunter from his back. The hunter held on tight and stabbed him in the shoulder. He howled in pain.

With her large teeth, Madelyn bit the hunter in the leg and yanked him from the white wolf's back. She didn't look back over her shoulder. "Go. Run and find the others."

"I'm fine. I'm not leaving you," Vincent grunted.

"No, you're not. You're bleeding. Now, go!"

"Maddie—"

"That's an order!"

He growled, but didn't question or object any further. Turning away, he ran out of the clearing.

The hunter, Jagger, got to his feet. "Oh well. One is better than none. Don't worry. I'll eventually get your friend."

Adjusting her stance, Madelyn snarled and charged at Jagger.

He side-stepped the lunge and changed the direction they faced. His unsettling forest-green eyes flicked back and forth as he watched and waited for her next move.

She approached him slowly. When she was close enough, she reared up on her back two legs to her full height and swiped at him with her claws.

He attempted to counter the move with his blade, but failed. Grimacing at the pain of the strike along his chest, he switched his knife to his other hand.

Settling back on all fours, she snarled and sprung at him. She knocked him to the ground and sent the blade skittering across the ground. By the time she spotted the other dagger, it was too late.

The hunter shoved Madelyn's wolf form from his body and stood. He stared down at the wolf lying on the ground.

Rolled onto her back, she gasped for air. The male had buried a knife deep in her gut.

A slow grin tugged at the corners of Jagger's mouth. He crouched down on his haunches and yanked his blade from the shapeshifter's belly. Dragging the knife across his black leather pants, he wiped away her blood and snickered. "Don't worry. Your friend may have gotten away, but I'll find them. Eventually, you all get what you deserve."

The shapeshifter took its last breath and its eyes rolled into the back of her head. As its heart stopped pumping, the light brown fur disappeared, its bones rearranged, and a naked woman formed where the wolf once lay.

With tears rolling down her cheeks, Grace gasped. The picture frame fell from her hands. Landing on the wooden floor, the glass shattered.

CHAPTER *eleven*

"GRACE?" VINCENT CLOSED the side door. He glanced over at the dining room. Her books laid open on the table, but she wasn't there. The breaking of glass in the back bedroom resounded loudly.

Oh no. No, no, no, no. Throwing his coat off, he darted down the hallway and stopped in the doorway of the one bedroom that had been off-limits. His gaze fell from her to the picture on the floor.

She lifted her tear-streaked eyes to him. "You knew."

It wasn't a question. It was a statement. But what did he know? He could see from the picture it was one of his pack taken a few weeks before Maddie's death.

"Jagger. He… he killed her… and you knew." Grace stared at him. Her eyes pleading with him that it was wrong. All wrong.

He heaved a deep sigh. His shoulders slumped. He'd do anything to give her the answer she wanted, but he couldn't. Vincent dropped his gaze to the ground. "Yes. I knew."

"And you said nothing."

"I wasn't sure how."

"Bullshit! You asked me question after question about Jagger, identified him as the one who broke into my apartment, and not once did you mention his involvement in my mother's death. Did you even try to find him afterward?" Grace sobbed. She closed her eyes and wrapped her arms around her body.

He had limited options after they'd found Maddie's body. They'd taken her body back to the shapeshifter campsite. Shapeshifters had their own police force to handle death notifications. Not long after that, his pack had cast him out.

He returned home and spent months searching for the hunter on his own. His parents helped where they could… until their own untimely death. Vincent stepped further into the bedroom. "It isn't that simple."

"It is that simple! Either you tried to find him or you didn't."

Gripping the back of his neck, he groaned inwardly. If only it had been one way or the other. In the end it had, but it hadn't lasted. "My pack kicked me out after that. They blamed me for Maddie… your mother's death. I did—"

"What about them? Where was the rest of the pack? Why weren't they around? Did they…" Her voice broke as her bottom lip trembled. She wept, her face getting splotchy by the second.

Damn it. Vincent rubbed at the ache in his chest. With two strides, he closed the distance between them and moved to wrap her in his arms.

"Don't touch me!" Grace backed up from him. "Because of you, she died alone!"

Lowering his hands to his sides, he winced at the verbal lashing. None of what she said was false, but it didn't make it any easier to hear. It also wasn't anything he could change. Maddie had skills most of the pack had only dreamed of. Jagger hadn't been the first hunter she'd taken on by herself, but he'd—

Vincent frowned. He shifted his gaze to Grace. All of her statements over the last two minutes replayed in his mind. It made little sense. She spoke as if she had been there, but that wasn't possible. "How do you know?"

"It doesn't matter." She stormed past him into the hallway.

Oh, no. She wouldn't get away without explaining herself. He chased after her and grabbed her by the elbow. "The hell it doesn't."

Grace yanked her arm free from his grip. "Why does it matter? Because you weren't the one to tell me when you should have? Or because she sacrificed her life for you."

"It matters because there are only two people who knew exactly what happened that night. As you pointed out, only *one* of them is still alive. And is also coming after *us*. Yes, it fucking matters." Vincent growled. His throat was thick with heat. His face tingled as his eyes narrowed. He was an asshole. Even if he made a valid point, he could've addressed the situation better.

Tears continued to fall from those champagne orbs of hers. Their natural light dimmed just a little. Grace's fists balled up. "Because I saw it, you selfish bastard! Just like I did with your parents and your first shift. I saw everything happen."

Vincent rubbed the top of his brow, propped his hands on his hips, and flicked his gaze to the ceiling. She did… who… what? He blinked. That wasn't the answer he expected. He thought someone had told her. Maybe Jagger had called her or one of his pack mates reached out. Hell, even Chip could've been an option.

This explained a lot. Why Maddie had never once mentioned Grace. Why she'd gone to such lengths to keep her out of the shapeshifter world. Exactly what her words to Chip meant. A shapeshifter kin with a third eye would completely change how they patrolled and located hunters. It would make her a formidable asset if anyone discovered her ability.

And as her mate, he was tasked with keeping her safe. Shit. He still hadn't told her anything about that. Oh, this day just got better and better. He regained his focus in time to hear the side door slam shut. Shit. Vincent ran the length of the hallway, through the kitchen and out of the house just as Grace drove off in his Lincoln.

"Son of a bitch!"

Grace sped off down Rose Hill. She didn't know where she was going, but she couldn't stay in that house one more second. Nothing was ever his fault. He didn't have to explain himself or his decisions, ever.

She was so fucking tired. Vincent's secrets had mentally and physically exhausted her. Now that the whole truth had come out, she'd give anything to go back to the night they met and change it all.

Jagger had been a pest, but he hadn't gotten violent until he'd seen her with Vincent. She'd been blessedly ignorant of the shapeshifter world, despite what her manuscript suggested. An unnamed mugger had been responsible for her mother's death. And her visions had belonged to no one except her.

All of that had gotten altered the night Vincent stepped into her father's antique store. Maybe that's where she could go. Her father wouldn't be at home. Right then, she just wanted—she didn't know anymore.

Grace wiped at the tears streaming down her face. What did she want? To hide? To be alone? No. She wanted answers. Vincent hadn't been the only one to hide the truth; her mother had too.

Taking the next right, she drove toward the one place where she expected to find clarity.

Sitting on the dark gray carpet of the spare bedroom in her childhood home, Grace scanned through the pictures she'd scattered across the floor. Her mother had stowed a couple of shoeboxes full of them. All the photographs were of her mother at various stages of her life and none of them included Grace or her father.

She didn't know any of the people in the pictures with her mother, which was exactly why she sat there. She clasped one photo in her hands and focused on it. Her mother had to be in her early twenties; she stood next to an older gentleman with one fountain in Washington State Park in the background.

Nothing. Damn it.

No matter how hard she concentrated on each new photograph she came across, she didn't get one vision. Why couldn't she call it when she needed it? No, it only showed up when she didn't want to see anything.

"It doesn't work like that."

Frozen to the ground, Grace swallowed. Nope. She didn't just hear her mother's voice. It was impossible. Her mother died eleven years ago. Shaking her head, she picked up another picture of her mother and a young woman—

"I told you 'it doesn't work like that.'"

Grace spun toward the voice. Her eyes widened as the photograph fell from her hand and fluttered to the floor. A woman who looked a hell of a lot like her mother stood a few feet away. She had the same caramel-colored hair swept into a ponytail, the same soft champagne eyes, the same jeans and t-shirt she always sported. Tears welled in the corners of Grace's eyes. "Mom?"

"Well, I'm certainly not your father."

Throwing the box of pictures aside, Grace jumped to her feet and threw her arms around her mother's solid shoulders. She wasn't hearing things. She wasn't seeing things. Her mother stood there in the flesh. "How's this possible?"

Her mother hugged her back. "Okay, don't get all teary-eyed on me. We don't have a lot of time."

What? No time? No. There had to be time. Taken aback, Grace released the hold she had on her mother. "I don't understand."

"I promise it'll all make sense soon." Cupping Grace's cheek, her mother sighed. "But you have to stop fighting your visions. They've been trying to tell you something, but you're my daughter and as stubborn as I was."

"But Mom, I don't want them. They have done nothing for me, except ruin everything." Her visions prevented her from having any genuine friends outside of Chip. They destroyed every relationship she'd ever had; her relationship with Vincent was its latest casualty.

"That isn't true. You and Vincent can still fix your problems. You just have to listen to one another. And your visions have helped with your father's store,

plus you've blossomed into a strong woman because of them. You just have to stop fighting them."

Grace narrowed her gaze. Her mother couldn't possibly know about any of that. The woman was dead, but she was seeing and talking to her. None of this made any sense. "How do you know about Vincent?"

"Oh, sweetie. I've always known. It's why I saved him." Her mother grabbed a hold of her hands and glanced over her shoulder. "Listen to me, go into the closet. On the floor is a pair of black boots. They have a small blade in a hidden pocket. Put them on. Go, now."

Her mother... she'd saved Vincent? No. That wasn't how she'd seen it. Grace shook her head and opened her mouth—

"Go! Now!"

With the blink of an eye, her mother was gone and Grace was still on the floor. Knocking the box of pictures from her lap, she got to her feet and glanced around the empty room.

She was alone.

It had to have been a vision, except she usually saw things that had happened in the past. She and her mother—the boots. Grace dug into the closet and quickly located the shoes her mother had referenced. Heading the worry in her mother's voice, Grace exchanged her sneakers for the gently worn black combat boots.

As she stood, she felt the cold steel against her right ankle and heard a rather distinct *click, click.* Neither of her parents had been fond of guns, but they had taught her to recognize their sound.

"Would you look... at... that! Of all the places I thought I'd find you, it wasn't here," Jagger said.

"What do you want?" Grace turned and faced her mother's murderer.

"A lot of things, but you'll do." His lips upturned into a harsh smile.

They had both needed space after their last fight, but almost nine hours had passed since Grace walked out and took off with his car. Vincent stared out of the backseat window. Despite the unanswered phone calls and text messages, he'd gotten into a taxi and tracked the GPS signal of his car.

It had last pinged by Grace's apartment, which made little sense. Derek and his crew hadn't started doing any work at her place. They hadn't even cleaned up.

The taxi slowed and pulled off to the side of the road. He handed the driver a couple of twenty-dollar bills and climbed out of the vehicle. Vincent glanced down both sides of the street and crossed with minimal traffic. It wasn't as busy this time of night as it would be on the weekend. This time of night, most people were getting ready for bed.

He ascended the staircase two at a time and paused halfway up. What the fuck? The front door to Grace's loft was open. Vincent peered over his shoulders. No one was around.

Tilting his head back, he sniffed the air. He smelled nothing honey scented and fresh moss didn't linger in the air. He only smelled the moss from the night before, intermingled with lavender. It was an interesting mix. He strode up the stairs the rest of the way and entered Grace's place.

Chip stepped out of the hallway, gun in hand, aimed right at the doorway. "Vincent?"

"For fuck's sake, put that down," he snapped. A bullet wouldn't kill him unless it was copper. Either way, it would do a hell of a lot of damage.

"Sorry. I didn't know it was you." Chip tucked the gun away in an inside jacket pocket. "What are you doing here?"

His gaze swept over the destruction of the apartment. There wasn't anything new. It all looked exactly as they'd left it last night. He shut the front door. "I'm looking for Grace. You?"

"The same."

"Have you heard from her at all?" Over the last week, he'd learned how close the two of them were. If she had turned to Chip after their fight, it wouldn't surprise him.

Chip rubbed his eyebrow. "No, and it's worrying me. I know she went to her parents' house. According to her father, the front door was open when he got home and there were old pictures of her mother all over the floor of the spare bedroom."

Old pictures? The front door had been opened? His gaze flitted from Chip to the destroyed living room and back again. He hooked his thumb over his shoulder to the front door. "Was this open when you got here?"

"Yes. Made me think whoever went looking for her at her parents' house found her here. She must've put up a fight, though." Chip gestured to the surrounding mess.

Damn it. Vincent pinched the bridge of his nose and shook his head. The one time he didn't immediately chase after her and she disappeared. Fuck. "This happened last night. Jagger did it before she got home. I had the door fixed, and she stayed with me last night."

"Then why don't you know where she is?"

Vincent opened his mouth just as his cell phone rang. He dug it out of his pocket. He saw Grace's face, exhaled a breath of relief, and answered the call. "Where the hell are you?"

"Careful Vincent. I don't want to kill your girlfriend here before you get the chance to try to save her."

A deep growl rumbled in his throat. "You touch one hair on her head and I'll rip your heart out."

"Oh! That sounds like fun," Jagger laughed manically.

"Where. Is. She." He punctuated each word as his grip tightened on the phone in his hand. He was going to kill that motherfucker if it was the last thing he did.

"Hunter Island. We'll be waiting." The line went dead.

"What the hell was that?" Chip asked.

"Jagger has her. I'll get her back. You deal with her father." Vincent shoved his cell back into his pocket and balled up his fists. It was a death trap, but he wouldn't fail her like he failed Maddie. This time he'd come with backup. Without waiting for Chip to agree to his terms, he spun on his heel and stormed out the door.

CHAPTER *Twelve*

HOW HAD SHE ended up here? Her feet were bound and her hands tied behind her back. Grace writhed, working to undo the rope around her wrists. If she could free herself, she could—she stilled at the sound of rustling leaves.

Jagger exited the tree line and brushed snow from his head. "Don't worry, Grace, this will all be over soon."

"You will be… once Vincent gets here." Unless she freed herself first. Then she'd take the steel blade hidden inside her boot and stab him in the gut like he'd done her mother.

He tossed his head back in laughter and crouched on his haunches. "It's cute that you think that atrocity could beat me."

"I know he can." She really shouldn't taunt the guy, but she couldn't stop herself, either. The bastard killed her mother. Still, it would be best if she kept her cool in case she couldn't take him by herself.

She'd witnessed part of the fight between him and Vincent, but from what she'd seen, Vincent hadn't been in his full form. If everything she believed was true, then he should be stronger, faster, and larger in his wolf form than his human one.

Sneering, Jagger rose to his feet and removed the gun he'd held on her earlier from his waistband. He dug a couple of copper bullets from the pocket of his pants and loaded the weapon. "He got away once. I don't plan on taking any chances this time."

Grace swallowed. This changed the playing field a little. She didn't know how copper would affect Vincent if he got shot, but getting shot could be deadly, period. She had to think. What could she… of course, that's it. If she had learned anything about Jagger, it was that he was extremely arrogant. All she had to do was play on it. Repressing a smile, Grace squinted and jutted out her chin. "Oh, I get it. You're scared to face him without a weapon."

"I'm not afraid of anything." Jagger snarled.

This was good. She just had to push back a little harder. "Of course you are, otherwise you wouldn't bother getting the gun ready."

Planting his feet firmly, he tucked the gun in the back waistband of his leather pants and crossed his arms. "I don't need it. I can beat him without it."

"Sure, you can." Her words dripped with sarcasm as she drew out the first word and gave him a dismissive nod. She shifted her gaze toward the forest. She wasn't looking at anything, but she had to convince Jagger of her belief in Vincent. The truth was… she didn't know what Vincent was capable of. She'd seen his complete wolf form one time. Well, three if she counted her visions. She had to believe it was enough.

Jagger scowled and scanned the nearby foliage. He stalked across the snow-covered ground and located a tree with a compact hole in its trunk. He took the small handheld gun from his waistband and place it inside the hole. "You'll see what I'm capable of. Once I've ridden this world of one more atrocity, you and I will have a little fun, then I'll kill you, like I did your mother."

Her narrowed eyes swung back to him. Her nostrils flared. She ground her jaw and forced the words down the back of her throat. The things she wanted to spew at him. Oh, how she wanted to cut off his balls.

Grinning widely, he closed the distance between them. "What? No comeback?"

"Untie me and I'll show *you* a comeback," she said through gritted teeth.

He backhanded her. "I'm done talking to you. Be quiet or the next one won't be so tender."

The slap jerked her head to the side. Grace unwound her jaw to ease the throbbing in her cheek and licked at the corner of her mouth. *Christ, that hurt.* The metallic taste of blood hit her tongue. Great, he'd split her lip open. She had pushed too far.

With a sneer, Jagger turned and faced the forest.

Then again, maybe it had been just enough. As quietly as she could muster, Grace returned to using the tree at her back to cut the rope from her wrists.

She didn't know how long it would take Vincent to get here, but she wouldn't let him go into the fight alone, either.

If she could help it.

He'd driven most of the way to Hunter Island, at least as far as he could. The rest he'd taken on foot. It hadn't been ideal, but he had to think of Grace. She couldn't shift like he could. His car sat a good quarter of a mile back.

Vincent scanned the forest again. Still no sight of his pack. He couldn't wait any longer. Lifting his muzzle to the air, he sniffed for Grace and darted toward her honey scent. It was stronger the closer he got. It also comingled with the smell of wet moss. A scent he was so ready to end.

He narrowed his gaze, searched the woods, and listened intently to everything going on around him. There was a slight rustle in the wind, along with a crinkling sound to his right. He shifted his eyes toward the minor noise. About a half mile off, he spotted Grace with her back against a tree, her hands behind her back and her feet bound.

Jagger stood close to where she sat, oblivious to whatever Grace was attempting. Or he pretended to be. A hunter's senses were more heightened than a normal human, although not as good as a shapeshifter's. This was truly a fight to live.

Without underestimating his opponent, Vincent came up with a plan of attack and ran forward. He burst out of the tree line and lunged at Jagger. He didn't go for the throat, but threw his shoulder into the hunter's gut and bit the arm that Jagger used to parry the charge.

Jagger slammed his fist into the side of Vincent's muzzle, which made him bite down harder until the bones snapped and he tasted blood. The hunter cried out and punched him again.

Vincent ripped his teeth from Jagger's skin. The man howled in pain as Vincent stepped back and spit out the chunk in his mouth. It was like swallowing sewer water. As much as he wanted to spare a glance at Grace, he couldn't take his eyes away from his opponent. Not without risking both their lives.

Hissing, Jagger withdrew a blade from a sheath hidden beneath his arm. He steadied his stance and tightened his grip on the knife's hilt.

He could go for the jugular, but he didn't want to give the hunter a chance to stab him. Vincent's gaze shifted to Jagger's other hand—the one holding the steel-tipped dagger. A low growl rumbled in his throat as he started circling the hunter.

Without missing a beat, Jagger moved in the same pattern. Both men eyed the other as they continued to encircle each other.

Rearing to his full height and standing on his hind legs, Vincent faked an attack from the right and swiped across the hunter's chest with his claws on the opposite paw.

Blood freckled Jagger's now-torn shirt. He kicked Vincent in the chest and sent him flying backwards into a tree.

His back slammed into the trunk with a loud crunch. The pain radiating up his spine momentarily stunned him. Slowly, he shook the daze from his body and got back to his feet. Vincent set his gaze on his prey, took aim, and charged the hunter.

Digging his elbows into his knees, Jagger got into a football stance and held tight to the knife in his hand. Dropping his shoulder low, he placed his good hand against the snow-covered ground.

The men crashed together as Jagger used his weight to flip Vincent over his head, who then landed on the cold, hard ground with a deafening thud behind him. Spinning around, he didn't give the man a chance to recover. He stabbed Vincent in the chest.

"No!" Grace cried out.

Vincent roared as the knife pierced his body a second time. He couldn't let Jagger get him a third. Barely getting any air in his lungs, he gathered all the strength he could muster and tossed the hunter back with his hind legs.

The blade skittered across the ground.

Grace watched in horror as Vincent attempted to get back up and failed. She glanced around to see where Jagger had landed and worked harder to free her wrists. She was close. The rope had frayed. Maybe—

Jagger slammed into the base of a tree several feet away. He grimaced and slowly ambled to his feet. Standing, he stumbled toward the tree where he'd tucked the gun away.

"No!" She gasped. Even as arrogant as he was, she should've known he wouldn't keep his word. She tugged at the strands wrapped around her wrists until they broke. With no time to spare, she grabbed the knife from her boot and cut the rope around her ankles.

Collecting the gun from the tree, Jagger cocked the weapon and faced Vincent, who'd gotten on his belly and sat partially up. Jagger shot him.

The bullet struck Vincent in the shoulder, knocking him onto his back. He grunted at the hit.

Completely free, Grace leaped to her feet. Before Jagger could get off another shot, she stabbed him in the back, plunging the blade as deep as it would go.

With a hiss, Jagger dropped the gun and swung wildly at Grace.

She dodged his half-assed punches and shoved him hard.

He fell and landed on his back, forcing the blade in deeper. Jagger groaned and coughed up blood.

Grace didn't stay to see what happened next. She kicked the gun out of the way, raced across the white ground, and skidded to a stop beside a naked Vincent. In the minute that had passed, he'd shifted from his wolf form to his human one. Tears rolled down her cheeks as she drank in his beaten and bruised body. She quickly removed her jacket and draped it across his chest, taking one of his hands in her own.

Vincent reached out and cupped her chin with his free hand. "You're okay."

"Yes, and so are you." She leaned ever so slightly into his touch. He had to get through this … to survive. Her cheeks grew wetter by the second. The veins where Vincent had gotten shot in his shoulder had changed to an unnatural green.

"Don't… cry." The normal command in his voice was gone. It had gone hoarse as he struggled to get the words out in one breath.

Shaking her head, Grace tightened her hold on his hand. He couldn't leave her. Not when everything was just starting for them. She peered over where Jagger still lay and then scanned the forest. There had to be something she could do. Maybe she could—

A gentle rustling caught her attention. Her gaze flicked toward the noise just as five massive creatures stepped out of the tree line: two wolves, two tigers, and one fox. Each of them with different colors.

Grace swallowed. She didn't have a weapon of any kind. Her knife was still in Jagger's back, Vincent was completely naked, and the gun… she didn't even know where it was, aside from nowhere nearby.

"Hey…" Vincent muttered.

She dropped her gaze to him and looked back at the creatures, focusing on each of their eyes. *The photograph.* This was her mother's pack… his pack. Tears rolled down her cheeks as relief washed over her. "Please, you have to help him."

One tiger with reddish yellow fur and black stripes approached. He nudged at her hand, the one holding onto Vincent. She blinked at him. Did he want her to let go? "No, I…"

Softening his green eyes, he nudged at her hand again, and then gave Vincent a gentle push with the top of his head.

Maybe he meant something else entirely. Biting the inside of her lip, she nodded, and with the help of the two wolves, she got Vincent atop the five-foot-tall tiger.

The other tiger with cinnamon-colored fur, slightly smaller in stature, kneeled down and glanced over his shoulder at his backside. With no further hesitation, she climbed up and held on tight. The two tigers darted into the woods with her and Vincent. The last thing she heard as they left was a blood-curdling shriek.

"Chip, Papa, I told you, I'm fine." She'd spent the last half-hour on the phone with the two of them, not that she'd left Vincent's side. As it turned out, Ethan and Amir were the ones to carry them back to the car that had gotten left a few miles from where they'd found her and Vincent. That he'd driven had proven quite useful.

She'd raced across town to the pack beta's home, as the male had directed. The beta, also known as Lucian, was a doctor. He'd removed the bullet from Vincent's shoulder and packed it with an herb to treat the poison from the copper bullet. Then stitched up the knife wounds, too.

That had been a few hours ago. Now, she sat in a lounge chair next to Vincent's bedside, their fingers laced together. She'd only called Chip and her father so they wouldn't freak out.

The room was pleasant, but not entirely sterile, as expected. The walls were a pale yellow. There was a light-redwood dresser against the far wall, a small matching nightstand, and a queen-sized bed with a sky-blue quilt.

A landscape painting hung above the headboard. The rest of the walls were bare.

"I'm glad to hear it. I can't tell you how worried I was about you," her father said.

"Same here, Grace. I expect that you'll give me a full account the next time we have lunch."

Not likely. It wasn't an experience she wanted to relive anytime in the foreseeable future. Maybe it was best she didn't share that with him; he'd just push harder to get it out of her. "Yep, sure thing."

"I thought we discussed this, Chip," her father said. "We won't pressure her into any decisions."

"I'm still her ward, in case you've forgotten."

"Ward schmord. I'm her father, and that carries more power."

With a light rap on the door, Ethan poked his fiery redhead into the bedroom. "We're ready."

Covering the mouthpiece of the phone with her hand, Grace sighed. "Is Lucian sure it's safe to move him?"

"Yes."

"Okay. Two minutes?" She had to get her family off the phone. Despite her earlier argument for taking Vincent back to the comforts of his own home, his pack and doctor had overridden her decision. According to them, girlfriend carried little weight. Either that or there was something else to the decision that she didn't comprehend.

Ethan gave her a curt nod and shut the door as he left.

"I have to go, you guys."

"Already?" Chip asked.

"But we've hardly spoken," her father tacked on. "We haven't had time to discuss your relationship with Vincent."

Mostly because she had gotten little of a word in edge-wise, but that was neither here nor there. "We're taking Vincent back to his house so he can recover there, and I told you I'm not talking about my relationship with you."

"Fine, but I expect you to call back as soon as you can. And once he's up and moving, I want a formal introduction."

"Yes, Papa. I will." She disconnected the call from her cell phone. One guy had gotten it back from Jagger… or his body, rather. It might be time for a new one.

Shifting her gaze to Vincent, Grace watched the rise and fall of his chest. He was alive. That was the most important thing right now.

Everything else, well, they could figure it out later.

CHAPTER *thirteen*

A SOFT BLANKET being laid over her arms startled Grace. She bolted upright in the chair she'd fallen asleep in and a little slice of light filtered in from the hallway. She regarded the fiery redhead hovering over her. "Ethan?"

"Yeah, sorry. I didn't mean to wake you." He smiled sheepishly.

She peered past his shoulder to the bed where Vincent still slept. A full twenty-four hours had passed, and he had yet to wake up. Shaking her head, she stretched her arms and readjusted in the chair. "I didn't know anyone else was here."

"We've all taken guard shifts."

Guard shifts? Taken aback, her eyes widened ever so slightly. Why would they need to be protected? Would another hunter come after them? "You don't think… I mean, we're safe, right?"

"Of course, but we don't take that chance when one of our own is healing and unable to protect his mate."

"Mate?" She blinked. It was the first time she'd heard the word. At least regarding Vincent. Was that why he'd pursued her the way he had?

Ethan dragged a hand through his hair. "I guess I shouldn't have said that."

"Why?" Yes, no one had mentioned it to her, but did that mean it was a secret? Not that it would be the first she and Vincent had kept from one another. Which was something that absolutely had to change.

"Well..." Ethan frowned. "He hasn't formally claimed you and he can't do that unless he rejoins the pack."

Interesting. This would all definitely have to be discussed. Although, they could always get married like normal humans do. Would it carry the same weight? Grace bit the inside of her cheek. He was a shapeshifter and there were certain traditions they didn't share—like Christmas. She'd minimally decorated her apartment, but his house hadn't gotten decorated for the holiday at all.

She opened her mouth and snapped it shut. How did she ask her question without sounding ignorant? Grace grimaced. What if they expected her lack of knowledge? She hadn't known about them, so it would stand to reason they hadn't known about her, either. "What if he doesn't want to go back? Could we still be mated?"

Tapping his index finger against his lips, his nose wrinkled. "I suppose it's possible, but it wouldn't hold the same recognition in our community."

"Like this protection detail," Grace stated. She didn't need him to acknowledge her comment to comprehend its truth. Everything about her world had changed, and she'd never be able to go back.

"Yes."

Flicking her eyes to Vincent, she stared at the bullet wound and the green coloring around the hole. Most of it had subsided from his veins, but not all of it. Regardless of what he did regarding the pack, she'd support him. She didn't care what tradition they followed as long as they were together.

He was worth it.

Her eyebrows knitted together as she returned her attention to Ethan. "What would it take for him to rejoin the pack?"

"We'd all have to agree to take him back, which would only occur if he accepted his punishment."

"Punishment? For what?" With all she'd learned about Vincent and why they'd kicked him out in the first place, neither of those statements made any sense.

"His involvement"—Ethan paused and gripped the back of his neck—"in your mother's death."

Grace held up a hand and silenced him. She wouldn't hear it. Not when she knew the truth, something they obviously didn't. "He isn't to blame. My mother sacrificed herself to protect him."

Ethan's jaw slackened. He crossed his arms and shook his head. "That makes no sense."

"Actually, it makes perfect sense." Her mother had told her to really look at all the visions she'd had. That's exactly what she'd done while trying to get her wrists free. She had finally paid attention.

To. Everything.

"You'll have to explain it to me. Before you do that, let me get Phillip."

Right. The alpha. Grace nodded. She had no problem telling them everything she'd discovered. Though she couldn't go into how, so she'd have to word it all carefully. Her gaze flicked briefly to Vincent. He deserved this chance. "Go ahead." She folded her arms across her chest, leaned back in her chair, adjusted the blanket, and draped one leg over the other. "I'll wait."

"Alright." Ethan gripped the back of his neck. "I'll… uh, I'll be right back."

Yet, he still stood here. Grace cocked an eyebrow at him. Did he require an armed escort? Silence stretched between them as she bounced her leg, impatiently waiting for him to leave. "Are you afraid he's going to bite?"

Ethan narrowed his green eyes at her. "No." With a smirk, he opened the door and exited the bedroom.

A little nudge and he did exactly as she wanted. Information she'd tuck away for later. It might come in handy down the line. She hadn't gotten to learn much about any of them. Something she should change over the coming days, but not right now. Her only focus was Vincent and what he needed. A knock sounded at the door, drawing her attention.

Before she could say anything, the door cracked open. Phillip poked his head in. "Ethan said you wanted to talk to me?"

"Yeah. About this… punishment that Vincent would have to accept if he wanted to rejoin the pack." Grace gestured for the alpha to enter the room further.

With a slight nod, Phillip slipped into the room and shut the door behind him. "He told you about that, huh?"

"Yes, he did."

"Did Ethan also share the circumstances?" Phillip propped up against the wall and crossed one ankle over the other.

"That's what I wanted to discuss because I think you've… misinterpreted what happened all those years ago."

His eyebrows furrowed. "I don't think I have, but explain."

Yeah, she knew he did, but *he* had to see that for himself. "I know you think Vincent just left my mother to fend for herself, but did you consider my mom's personality?" Grace uncrossed her leg and leaned forward, pressing her elbows into her knees. "My mother was a protector. That's what an alpha does, right? They don't just lead, but they protect their pack."

"Yes. That doesn't change the facts. It was Vincent's responsibility to stay with her. We hunt together for a reason."

Valid point. How did she argue against that? She couldn't tell him she knew the truth. Maybe she could convince him of another possibility. "What if she believed Vincent had more to live for? That his survival mattered more than her own. I believe that's why she sent him away. She would've done the same thing if it was any of you." Grace lifted a hand, silencing him. "Yes, I know she still had me and my father, but if she thought the survival of her pack outweighed her own, then she would've taken the risk. My mother always put others before herself. I imagine you've done the same thing from time-to-time."

His jaw clenched, and he blew out a heavy breath. "Occasionally."

"Then don't you think you should reconsider your stance? I mean, if she decided and gave him an order, then why fault him for her choice?" If the slight glint in his eyes was anything to go by, then she had him exactly where she wanted. He had to reconsider everything that had happened eleven years ago, but she had to be certain. "Look, I don't know what kind of alpha my mother was, but I know her. Maybe she believed she could beat Jagger alone. Even if she didn't, I know she would've done whatever she had to do to protect whoever was with her."

With the dip of his chin, Phillip pushed off the wall. "I'll discuss this with the pack, but I won't guarantee anything changes."

"I wasn't asking for that; just the reconsideration. Though I believe you'll all do the right thing. Not because of who I am or who my mother was to you, but because it's what Vincent deserves." He'd survived all this time without his family, his pack. She wanted to give that back to him. And she believed she'd done just that.

Vincent groaned in silence and attempted to open his eyes. The twinge in his chest and throbbing in his shoulder threatened to pull him back under. All the sensations wracking his body reminded him that he was alive. That was the best feeling ever.

Grace!

She'd still been tied to the tree. No. Wait. That wasn't right. Damn it. Why couldn't he get his eyes to cooperate? The soft sound of breathing tickled his ears. Maybe he couldn't see, but he could hear. He listened, focusing intently on the steady breaths escaping the person's tiny nostrils.

It was Grace. His Grace.

A slow smile tugged at the corners of his mouth. She was there—with him. He patted along the blanket beneath his hand and tried again to open his eyes. Slowly, his eyes fluttered open. He could see her caramel hair in a tangled mess, her eyebrows knitted together, and her rosy lips pursed tight. She must be having some kind of dream. He didn't want to wake her, but he needed to feel her, even if it was just her hand.

"Grace," he croaked out. Was that really him? His voice? Christ, how long had he been out to sound like a frog?

Tossing the blanket aside, she bolted upright. Her gaze flitted back and forth as her eyes bounced all around the room. Stifling a yawn, she looked over at Vincent. "You're awake!"

He tried to sit up, but his shoulder screamed at him. With a grunt, Vincent laid back against the pillows. The bullet may not have pierced any major organs, but the copper from it had obviously done some damage.

Closing some of the distance between them, Grace clasped his hand and stroked the top of his head. "Don't move too much. Your body is still healing."

"How long…" he asked hoarsely. He couldn't finish the entire question without sounding less like a man. He was supposed to be the one taking care of her, not the other way around.

"Two days. You've been out for two days." She squeezed his hand as tears welled in the corners of her eyes and rolled down her cheeks. "Oh God, I'm crying. I'm sorry… I don't know why—"

"It's okay. We're okay." He cupped her chin and brushed the tears off her face. She didn't have to explain. Back in the forest, when he'd seen Jagger go for the gun, he'd thought it was all over. For both of them. It didn't matter if he died, but he had to keep fighting to protect her. In the end, she'd saved him.

Tugging on her hand, he opened up his arms. Maybe he couldn't sit up, but it didn't mean he couldn't hold her. They were in the privacy of his bedroom, exactly as they'd left it before their last fight.

She dug her elbow into the mattress, maintaining space between the two of them. "Let me get Lucian first."

"For what? I'm—"

The bedroom door flew open. Amir appeared in the doorway, his dark hair tousled as he scanned the room, gun in hand. Tucking the weapon away, his gaze shifted from Grace to Vincent. He crossed his arms. "About time you woke up."

Vincent smirked. He was grateful to see his former packmate here. If nothing else, it meant they'd kept their promise, which also meant they were probably the ones who helped get him home. It didn't mean they had welcomed him back into the fold, but his family had been there when he needed them most. "I'll remember that the next time one of us gets shot."

"I don't envy you there," Amir snickered. Turning his attention to Grace, he hooked a thumb over his shoulder. "I'll let Lucian know."

"Thank you, Amir." Grace's champagne eyes softened with a tender smile.

"You're welcome." With a tiny bow of his head, Amir backed out of the bedroom and shut the door behind him as he exited.

Raising an eyebrow, Vincent glanced from the closed door to Grace and back again. Had some kind of silent exchange occurred between them? It seemed as if they had said something to one another. "Are you sure it's only been two days?"

"Yes, absolutely. Why?" She tilted her head to the side.

"Because he deferred to you." He frowned. Didn't she understand the importance of what had just happened? Only three kinds of people warranted the respect Amir had shown: elders, alphas, and *mates*. They hadn't even spoken about that.

Not yet.

With everything else that had occurred, there hadn't been time. Not to mention, he didn't want to scare her off. Losing her had become his number one fear.

Beaming, Grace leaned in close. "Let's just say I've had a long conversation with your entire pack."

His pack? Vincent blinked. They hadn't belonged to him in years. What would make her say that? Unless… no, she couldn't have. Maybe? She had visions. Although he didn't quite understand what all that entailed, could it have something to do with the change? There were too many questions running through his head. He rubbed at his temple. "Explain."

"I helped them see the truth. They know you aren't responsible for my mother's death, and if you're willing, they'd like you to rejoin them."

Two words he never thought he'd hear. Obviously, it would hold the most weight once he heard it from Phillip. But the knowledge that it was even a possibility... that was enough. He lifted Grace's hand to his mouth and pressed a gentle kiss to her palm. "I hope this means we have a future together."

A bright smile fell to her lips as her eyes lit up the entire room. "I'd like that. We have a lot to figure out, but I believe in us. Can we just promise each other one thing?"

"Anything." Whatever she wanted; it was hers. He'd move the moon if she asked him to or die trying.

"No more secrets."

After everything they'd been through to get where they were, he could do that. The rest would fall into place. "I can do that. I promise you, my mate, no more secrets."

Grace bit her bottom lip. Pure bliss radiated out of her as her champagne eyes shined and she brushed a soft kiss across his lips. "I like the sound of that."

His heart swelled with joy as his whole body relaxed. Whatever pain he'd felt a few minutes ago disappeared. Everything in his world was finally right. Vincent's grin faltered. One thing nagged at him in the back of his mind. "What about your father?"

"Well..." Grace paused, the warmth never leaving her soft features. "He's agreed to give you a chance, but he has requested a formal introduction."

Vincent chuckled and winced at the ache in his shoulder. Still, he wouldn't trade it for anything in the world. "I think we can arrange that."

There was a slight rap on the door, and then Lucian poked his head in. "I'm not interrupting, am I?"

"Not at all. Come on in," Grace said.

"I see our patient has finally come around." A faint smirk crossed Lucian's features. "You had us worried for a second."

"You know nothing can keep me down." Vincent flashed a half-hearted grin.

"Not something you had to prove." The male shut the door and strode across the room. Leaving over, he lifted the bandage on Vincent's shoulder. "This looks a lot better."

He eyed the injury out of his periphery. It didn't look too bad. Most of the putrid green veins had dissipated, which meant he was on the mend. Grunting, Vincent struggled to sit up. His shoulder hollered, throbbing with every move he made. Though it didn't deter him. He needed to hold his mate. "Good. Then I can get out of bed."

"Don't be a fool. You're still recovering." Lucian slid the blanket aside and gently prodded his fingers along the scar lining Vincent's left pectoral. "This has mostly healed, but that gunshot wound will take longer."

"He's right," Grace agreed. "There's no need to rush into anything. Just rest."

"For how long?" He couldn't lay in bed forever. Even if her father hadn't demanded a formal introduction, he needed to do that. After he got her in his arms. He needed to feel her close to him. Much closer than she was currently.

"However long it takes," Lucian declared. The male folded his arms across his chest. "I patched you up, but you know how harmful copper is to us. Take it easy. We're taking turns on guard duty until you're one hundred percent. Okay?"

His family really had come through for him. As much as he loathed laying there, doing nothing, he couldn't argue too much with the male or what his body demanded of him. Reluctantly, Vincent conceded. "Alright."

"I'm glad you see things my way." The corner of Lucian's mouth curled. He dipped his chin at Grace. "Everything looks wonderful, so I'll give you both some privacy."

"Thank you, Lucian."

"Of course." With a slight bow of his head, the male left the bedroom and shut the door behind him.

Another of his packmates deferred to her. A day he never thought he'd see. Vincent's gaze settled on Grace. "You really have a way with them."

"I don't know about that." Her eyebrows knitted together. "I think we've just found… mutual respect."

That's not how he saw it, but none of that mattered at the moment. He caressed her cheek. "Since the doctor has given an all-clear, does this mean you'll lay down with me?"

"If I do, will you rest?"

While he wouldn't guarantee sleep, he would stop trying to move around so much. "Yes."

Grace nodded. She stood, walked around to the other side of the bed, and crawled in next to him. Settling her flush against his side, he gingerly ran his fingers across her hip. If he had to be stuck in bed, this was the only way he wanted to do it. With the world at his fingertips.

CHAPTER fourteen

VINCENT STARED AT the peach door. It was just a door. That wasn't true. It was a door that could forever alter his future. It had been two days since he'd woken up in his bedroom. After Lucian had left, he and Grace talked about everything. He learned more about her visions, even the presumption that her mother had them, and he admitted to what led him to search for her.

All of their secrets were out in the open. At least with one another.

That wasn't what had him on the man's doorstep this evening, but it had everything to do with Grace. As she had advised him, his pack asked him to rejoin their ranks. *That* was part of what brought him here. A small part. The other… he inhaled and exhaled a deep breath. Hesitantly, he knocked on the door.

A good minute passed without an answer. He didn't hear any movement on the other side, either. Vincent lifted his hand to knock on the door again, and it opened.

Grace's father stood on the other side and narrowed his dark brown eyes at him. "What're you doing here?"

"I wanted to talk to you, Mr. Reddington." Normally, he would've taken the man out to dinner for a conversation of this magnitude. However, the guy didn't care for him much, so he suspected dinner was out of the question. Although he would have dinner with the man in a couple of nights since Grace had planned it.

"About?"

Well… this was off to a great start. Vincent gripped the back of his neck and attempted to release the tension building in his body. "It's important. Could we discuss it inside?"

Crossing his arms, Grace's father grunted and stepped aside. "I suppose."

One barrier down. How many more would he have to go through? He couldn't say, but it would be worth it in the end. Politely bowing his head to the man, Vincent strode past his mate's father and into the man's dwelling.

The house was simple. A single-story ranch-style home with wooden floors everywhere except the bedrooms. From the foyer, he surveyed the various rooms. The living room, to his right, had a gray sectional couch, a glass antique coffee table, two matching end tables and a 40-inch T.V. mounted on the wall. The dining room, to his left, had a dark antique-oak square table seating six. It had a rather classic but comfortable look. The kitchen sat just beyond the dining room with a nice island as its central component. "You have a beautiful home, Mr. Reddington."

"Thank you," the old man said as he shut the door. He waltzed by Vincent and headed straight for the kitchen. "Now, what was so important that you had to come over here and interrupt my dinner?"

Grace's father was a ratchet old man. He wondered if the man had always been like that or if it was just since Maddie died. If he'd been that way for a while, then Maddie was a saint for putting up with it. He didn't expect that was the case. Vincent entered the kitchen and sat on one of the bar stools at the breakfast bar. "I apologize for showing up like this, but I wanted to talk to you about mine and Grace's relationship."

"My daughter told me you two were dating. I don't like it, but I can't force her hand. As long as you don't hurt her, we'll be okay."

Her father didn't like it? Vincent thought back to the day he'd overheard the old man say "his kind." Pursing his lips, he rubbed his eyebrow with his thumb. "Do you disapprove because I'm a shapeshifter?"

The old man turned on the stool and faced Vincent. He scowled. "Your damn right I do. My wife, God rest her soul, died protecting Grace from your world, yet you've dragged her into it."

"It was your wife's world, too." Over the last few days, he and Grace had spoken extensively about the shapeshifter community, as well as the pack. They'd come to a few decisions. No one would be told about her visions, not even her father. Her father would never be told that he was a member of her mother's pack. Nor would they ever disclose the accurate details of Maddie's death.

"I know that, but we agreed Grace would never know about it. Yet, here we are. She doesn't just know about it, she got nabbed by a hunter, and she's dating a shapeshifter." Pinching the bridge of his nose, Grace's father sighed and picked the fork up from his plate.

Vincent sat up straight. There were some things he couldn't reveal, but that didn't mean he couldn't make certain reassurances. "Mr. Reddington, I understand your reluctance. I promise you, Grace is well protected. She doesn't just have me watching her back, but she also has my pack, too. I love her very much, and I'll do everything in my power to make sure she always knows that and that she's safe and taken care of. That's why..." he paused and swallowed to check his nerves. "I'd like your permission to make her my mate."

The fork fell from the old man's hand. It clattered against the plate. "You want to mate, my daughter?"

"Yes. Although I want to do it in the shapeshifter way, I'd also like to marry her in the human way," Vincent said. According to shapeshifter laws, he didn't have to get her father's blessing. That right belonged to her ward. While he would have this same conversation with Chip, it seemed more important to begin with the man who helped give Grace life.

Grace's father sat there in silence as he stared at the plate of mashed potatoes, green beans, and ham that the male had heated. The old man said nothing for a few minutes. He just eyed the food as if it had been freshly placed in front of him.

He didn't want to push, but the man hadn't moved. "Mr. Reddington?"

"I'm thinking." Grace's father waved his hand dismissively. He picked his fork back up and had a bite of green beans. Another minute passed before he faced Vincent. "What do you love about her?"

"Her kind heart; she's always putting someone else first. Her ambitions; I think she'll make a great social worker one day. The way she takes care of her friends and family. Grace is more than just a beautiful woman; she has a gorgeous soul." A week ago, he may not have been able to answer that question. But deep down, he'd known since that first night they met they belonged together.

The old man's head bobbed up and down. He set the fork aside. "It takes a lot of guts to come to a woman's father, especially when you know he doesn't like you, and ask for her hand." He sighed. "I would never stand in the way of Grace's happiness. But what would you do if I said 'no?'"

Vincent's shoulders slumped. "Then I would do everything to prove to you I'm a good man. A man that deserves her."

"Well, damn. That's an excellent answer, son." Grace's father faced him and held out his hand. "You have my blessing."

Grace stood back and eyed the six-foot tree she and Vincent had just finished decorating. He sat on the floor and fumbled with the string of lights, attempting to get it plugged in and on.

"Damn it." Vincent shook his finger. With another grunt, the lights flickered and came to life. He crawled out from under the tree.

She smiled at the way the white bulbs complemented all the red and blue ornaments and the pinecones. It even highlighted the silver tinsel they had used sparingly. The tree was perfect in its simple decorations.

"You're right. It makes it a little homier in here," Vincent said, draping an arm around her shoulders.

"Yes, it does, and it just needs one final touch." She turned and snagged the deep blue tree skirt she'd picked up the day before. Getting on the floor, Grace wrapped the skirt around the legs of the tree stand. She got back to her feet and faced Vincent.

Her eyes widened at the sight of him down on one knee, holding a small black box in his hand. Her fingers touched her parted lips as she stifled a gasp.

"I know tomorrow's Christmas and gifts are normally presented then, but I couldn't wait." A broad smile spread across his mouth. "We talked about getting mated in my tradition, but we're two halves of a whole. I'd like to be your mate and your husband, if you'll have me."

Vincent lifted the top of the black box. Inside the purple velvet sat the most stunning ring she'd ever seen. A halo of diamonds surrounded a round-cut, sparkling rose stone. The gem sat atop a white gold band, which was accented by more diamonds.

Tears prickled the corners of her eyes. She couldn't believe this was happening. They hadn't been together long, but she needed little time to know they were meant to be. Her mother had known. She'd finally understood that was why the woman had sacrificed herself eleven years ago.

So that she could have a future with this man. This wonderful, supportive, loving man before her. Grace bit her bottom lip. "Yes."

Beaming, Vincent jumped to his feet, slipped the ring on her ring finger, and pressed his lips to hers. He hugged her tight, lifting her off the ground as he spun her around. "I love you so much."

"I love you too." She laughed at his excitement. None of this was what she thought would happen when she turned him down the first time he'd asked her out. Her entire world changed the day he walked into her father's store. For the better. Although it didn't seem like it at first. Of all the decisions she'd ever made in her life, she was grateful she had a friend who pushed her to take one more leap.

Because it was the leap of a lifetime. When Vincent set her back on her feet, she kissed him again. "Since we're exchanging gifts, I have one for you, too."

"What? You didn't have to get me anything."

"I know, but I wanted to." Grace reached over to the box she'd carried the tree skirt in and pulled out a dark wood picture frame. The edges of the frame had an intricate design that had been hand-crafted. She had planned to wrap it but now seemed like the right time to give it to Vincent. Her gaze drifted over the picture of her mother and the pack one last time before she handed it to him.

His eyes dropped to the reframed photograph and shifted back to her. He swallowed. "I didn't… when did you… how did you…"

"I found the broken one tucked away in your closet the other day." She laced her fingers together, the ring on her finger a new sensation she'd have to get accustomed to. "I thought it deserved to be displayed."

"Thank you." His lips found hers once more.

"Grace?" Vincent called out. She had this blank stare. The pencil fell from her fingers. What the hell? He waved his hand in front of her face. Still, she didn't respond or react. Jumping to his feet, he knocked his chair over, crouched down on his haunches, and gripped her hand. Was she having a vision? He hadn't seen it happen yet, but she'd told him that she'd had at least one since they'd gotten together. She had a vision of his first transformation. All he recalled was the far-off look she'd gotten. It was similar to this one.

Grace gasped. Tears welled in the corners of her eyes as their gazes met. She threw her arms around his neck, grasping tightly to him.

"Hey. It's alright. I've got you." Despite the hold she had on him, she shook with violent sobs. Whatever she'd seen cut her deep. What could it be? Wrapping an arm around her waist, he scooped her up and lifted her out of the chair. It seemed like a good idea to get her away from the dining room table.

"No, it's not," she choked out.

"Why don't you tell me about it and we can figure it out together?" He carried her over to the couch, sat down, and got comfortable with her flush against his side. Pressing a kiss to her forehead, he rubbed slow circles along her back. This was partially why they had mentioned nothing of her visions to his pack. Grace didn't have full control of them. Until they figured out how best to use what she saw, it made little sense to share anything.

"They were after us," she whispered against his chest.

"Who was?" That didn't give him much to work with. They were bound to cross paths with other hunters. Vampires and witches left them alone as long as they stayed out of their territory. That only left humans, except most of them believed the supernatural were nothing more than a myth.

"I don't know."

That helped even less. Maybe since her breathing had settled, he could get more details out of her. Vincent brushed the tears from her cheeks, placed a finger beneath her chin, and lifted her eyes to meet his. "Tell me what you saw."

With a slight nod, Grace inhaled and exhaled a deep breath. She wiped the last of the tears from her face. "We were in a hotel. Our names and photos flashed across the television screen. I grabbed a bag to pack when you said they found us and we had to go. You grabbed my hand, tugged me toward the door, opened it, and then I snapped back to here."

Vincent frowned as his eyebrows knitted together. That didn't make a lick of sense. Why would they appear on the television? Who could he have referred to? "I thought you didn't see the future."

"I never have before, but maybe it's changed." Grace snuggled against him. "If that's not the case, then what else could this mean?"

That was a damn good question. One he wished he could answer. Because what she'd described wasn't something that had happened, which meant it had to be the future. At least something that could happen. Or a warning? But to what? He rubbed his thumb across his brow. "I don't know, but we'll figure it out." They didn't have any other choice.

Grace stood in front of the full-length mirror in Vincent's bedroom, soon-to-be *their* bedroom. It had been a week since he'd proposed, and she'd already packed up whatever hadn't broken back at her place. She'd suggested to her father that he put it up for rent.

She stared at her reflection in the mirror and brushed her hands down the sparkling beaded-and-sequined bodice that hugged her natural curves. The dress was sleeveless with a high neckline that closed at the back, and it had an A-line cut. Her hands continued to the chiffon, knee-length skirting. It was quite beautiful and perfect for the combined party—New Year's Eve and Vincent's birthday. She'd even pinned her hair up for the occasion.

"Wow," Vincent said from the doorway. "You look stunning."

Peering over her shoulder, Grace smiled and licked her lips as her gaze raked over him from head to toe. He looked quite yummy in his black tuxedo. The way the tailored suit fit his broad shoulders. Or how the lustrous satin lapel stretched across his muscular chest. The crisp white button-up and tie at his throat left a lot to the imagination, although she'd seen it all. The pants were taut against his powerful legs. "I'm not the only one."

A low growl rumbled in his throat as he strode across the room. He pressed a tender kiss to her lips and wrapped her in his arms. "I'm going to enjoy peeling this dress off of you later."

"Mm, I like the sound of that, but first we have a party to get to." She slid her hand into his and threaded their fingers together. They didn't want to be late.

"Actually, before we go, I need to tell you about the phone call I just took."

Her eyebrows knitted together. His phone had gone off a few minutes earlier—it had been from his office. But how would that involve her… unless they'd selected a winner? She swallowed. "Oh?"

The corner of his lips tugged into a small smile. "You won the contest."

That's what she thought he'd say. Her vision from the other day replayed in her mind.

"Are you sure they can't find us here?" Grace asked as she snuggled a little deeper against her mate.

Vincent pressed a tender kiss into her hair. "I promise you, we're safe."

Her gaze flicked to the news channel they'd watched for the last twenty minutes. It was the only way to monitor things. "This just in. The police are hunting for these two suspects connected with the murder of a local judge," the news anchor said. Two photographs flashed across the television screen.

"What the hell?" Grace's eyes widened as she bolted upright. They weren't safe. Far from it if the police were looking for them. She glanced at her mate. "Please tell me I'm seeing things."

He opened his mouth and snapped it shut. Jumping to his feet, Vincent peered at the window. They'd fully drawn the curtains closed upon their arrival. Although he stared at it, she didn't think he could see anything. Still, he didn't move.

She couldn't sit there and do nothing. Grace stood, gathered their bag and clothes out of the closet, and started packing. Their pictures were all over the news. They couldn't stay.

"There's no time. They're here." Vincent raced around the bed, grabbed her hand, and dragged her toward the door.

"What? That's not possible."

"Come on. We need to go now." He yanked the hotel door open.

Despite all they'd talked about regarding her vision, she'd only drawn one conclusion. That only one thing led them down that path. Grace inhaled and exhaled a deep breath. It left her with one choice. "I'm not going to accept it."

He grimaced as he rubbed his forehead. "What? Why?"

"You remember the vision I told you about the other day?" Fidgeting, she walked away. Her heels clicked against the wooden floor as she headed over to the bed.

"Yeah, but what does that..." He paused and gripped the back of his neck with a heavy sigh. "You can't think it has something to do with the contest."

She nodded and wrapped her arms around her waist. "That's all I can think. I know you don't want to believe we were running from something, but we were. It could only stem from this."

Vincent crossed the room in two long strides. He cupped her chin. "Listen to me. There are so many possibilities and nothing is set in stone. Even if you turn this down, it doesn't mean your vision won't come to pass."

Her gaze lifted to his. She'd already given this a lot of thought. Yes, it was a work of fiction, except it wasn't. Although she'd changed the names, it would draw too much light on their world. The consequences of that happening were far too great. "Maybe you're right, but what if you're not? I won't take that risk. The book, the money, none of it is worth that. So, I'm going to decline."

Stroking his thumb across her cheek, a small smile played on his lips. "I don't know what I did to deserve a woman like you, Grace Reddington, but I'm glad I have you in my life."

"Me too." He had given her novel a chance. That mattered a lot to her. It put the decision back into her hands.

Vincent pressed a gentle kiss to her forehead and made his way over to the closet. He reached to the top shelf and retrieved a box wrapped in silver paper. "Well, I had a congratulations gift for you, but I suppose this could be a thank-you gift."

"Thank you? For what?"

"For making a tough decision." He held out the small, square-shaped box.

She cracked a grin as she accepted it. Carefully unwrapping it, she set the paper aside on the bed and opened the top. Her eyes widened as she removed a glass-covered, intricately constructed rose bud with a dark wooden base. Four words had been inscribed on the front of the base: *Grace, you're my forever.* She blinked back tears. "This is beautiful."

"I'm glad you like it."

Grace set the case on the dresser. Later, she'd move it to the mantel where it could always be seen. She closed the distance between her and her fiancée and hooked her arms around his neck. She brushed a loving kiss across his lips. "It's perfect. You're my forever, too."

Soon enough, they'd get married in both of their traditions and everyone else would know it as well. Regardless of her vision, she felt the truth in her bones. They had a beautiful life ahead of them. One where they got to live happily ever after.

Or so she hoped.

The End

ABOUT THE AUTHOR

Author of the Love's Worth Series, BRIGIT ROSÉ lives in a world of romance. She has taken her life experience and made it into one endless love story. When she's not writing, she's singing loudly and off-key, hanging out with friends, or playing with her 2.5 fur babies. She can usually be found with a kiss in one hand and a twist of line in the other, exactly the stories she likes to read and write. If you'd like to know more about Brigit, you can find out more on her website: HTTPS://KBFENNERROSE.COM.

OTHER WORKS BY BRIGIT ROSÉ

LOVE'S WORTH SERIES

UnHinged

ReIgnited

THE MYSTIC CHRONICLES

Detached

Co-authored

PRISMA ISLE SERIES

Perfectly Reckless

Chaotic Tranquility

Rebel Tides

Under Krys Fenner

DARK ROAD SERIES

Addicted

Damaged

Avenged

Burned

Twisted

THE GUARDHIAN SERIES

Awakened

Disillusioned

COMING SOON

Betrayed (Dark Road Series)
ReUnited (Love's Worth Series)
Shattered Wonderland (The Lucent Chronicles)
Wicked Ground (The Arcarean Academy)
Inherited (The Guardhian Series)
Siren's Curse (Prisma Isle Series)

Made in the USA
Middletown, DE
15 May 2024